The dead warrior sat holding his weapons, staring with unblinking ice-gray eyes.

There was something different about him, a feeling that he was not dead, though he certainly looked to be. No man could survive a winter in the heights without food or shelter, yet there was no sign that a fire had ever been made here. Still there was something about the warrior . . . Timidly, Hogar reached out a hand to touch the cheek of the man who had saved them from the bandits.

He jerked his hand back as if it had been burned. The skin should have been hard as a rock, yet there was an odd suppleness to it, in spite of the chill that lay behind the gray unmoving flesh . . .

Charter Books by Barry Sadler

CASCA:
THE SENTINEL

#9

BARRY
SADLER

C

CHARTER BOOKS, NEW YORK

CASCA #9: THE SENTINEL

A Charter Book / published by arrangement with
the author

PRINTING HISTORY
Charter Original / October 1983

ISBN: 0-441-09237-3

Charter Books are published by The Berkley Publishing Group,
200 Madison Avenue, New York, N.Y. 10016
PRINTED IN THE UNITED STATES OF AMERICA

CHAPTER ONE

The Brotherhood

To Constantinople came riders of horses of noble blood. Others came in the rags of beggars or the robes of merchant princes, nobles from the courts of Persia in cloth of gold and silver. Men of power, privy to the councils of the great men of the world, all rode to Constantinople, the last great city of the Caesars. The word had been sent, and they would obey. This was the conclave set for the most holy of days, to celebrate the death of the lord Jesus Christ and to reaffirm their faith and devotion to the teachings of the prophet Izram, the thirteenth disciple.

From all the known world they came, these men of many coats, all dedicated to one purpose in life. No matter what their station in the secular world, there was no greater order than that of the Brotherhood of the Lamb. A man might be a prince in his own land, but one who was a beggar might be his master in the Brotherhood. All would serve their purpose as ordained by the Elder. Therefore, they rode or sailed by ship or walked the long trails and roads that led to the capital city of the Eastern Empire, indeed now the only empire left of what had been the glory of Rome.

Constantinople was more Greek than Latin. The speech of the court and the manner of dress were a mixture of Greece and the decadent East. Opulent wealth and unbelievable poverty walked hand in hand on the streets.

The Elder was anxious, awaiting the conclave that would happen this night. There was much to be done and many things to decide upon concerning their next course of action. They had

1

done well in the last hundred years. They, more than the Goths or Huns, had brought Rome to her knees. For they were the instrument that had to destroy the rising influence of the Catholic Church. That meant Rome had to be destroyed to slow the spread of the false teachings of those who called themselves Catholic.

It was their influence that had brought about the uprising of the Goths, and it was their hand that had arranged the death of Rome's ablest general, Stilicho, when it looked as if he might be too successful in restoring the might of Rome after driving the Huns out, and it was they who had persuaded the emperor of the East to send only token aid to his brother emperor, and then always too late to do any real good.

Only in a state of chaos could the new order be established, and the greatest threat to their influence was the church of Rome. The barbarians would be dealt with in time. That was one thing they didn't worry about, for they were prepared to spend centuries to accomplish their mission. They were patient. The Elder knew that their day would come, but the time was not yet. There was much to be done in their holy mission.

They had to prepare themselves for the second coming of Jesus, and they had lost the road to him. It had to be found again— that was the purpose of this grand conclave. The road must be found again so that they could be at the right place when the Lamb chose to return.

They, and only they, knew the truth of that day at Golgotha. Theirs was the great secret, not to be shared with those outside their order, for they were the followers of the thirteenth disciple, Izram the Syrian.

Izram had stated that there must be chaos before there could be order, and it was their holy duty to create that condition. The world must be in turmoil. Jesus could come at any time, and they had to be ready.

The Elder smiled under the hood of his plain homespun robe of rough wool. Chaos and disorder! Rome survived a thousand years, and we destroyed her in fifty. Fewer than a thousand of us have brought down the city of the Caesars. Because of us, a barbarian rules in Rome and the Catholic Church has been set back a hundred years.

Odoacer, a barbarian general, took the last reins of power into his own hand and made himself king of Italy after deposing Romulus Augustus, the last emperor of the West, not knowing that he was only a tool that would be broken when he no longer served his purpose for the Brotherhood.

Persia, too, had been reduced as a power through their judicious use of treachery. At a critical moment in battle against the White Huns near the borders of Kushan, an arrow had found its way into the heart of the Persian king. With his death, the Persian army had lost heart, and the White Huns slaughtered them to a man. Nomads were the masters of the Sassanids, and it would be a long time before the empire of the Persians breathed freely again.

It was easier to deal with barbarians. Their minds were so simple and obvious. Already, in order to prevent the rise of a civilized empire of the White Huns in Persia, they had arranged to turn their interests toward the wealth of India and away from the West. Only Constantinople remained as a truly great power, and for now they needed the city and its armies. By their will the Eastern Empire would survive a while longer.

In this, the year *A.D.* 485, the Brotherhood was alive and well save for the lost road, and that they would find again, though it might take a hundred years.

An acolyte brought a torch to light the Elder's way from his rooms in the palace to the catacombs and huge cisterns beneath the streets of Constantinople. In one of these huge chambers the Brotherhood would meet and reenact the crucifixion as they had done on this day ever since the death of their master at the hands of the beast.

The Elder was weary from his labors but not dissatisfied, for was he not the comites (supervisor of offices) for the emperor? He did regret slightly the fact that he'd had to become a eunuch in order to gain such a position of influence. However, that small sack of flesh was as nothing to him, for now it was he who approved the candidates for most of the important offices of the empire. He could place whom he wished where he wished and thus control the destiny of millions.

He inspected the chamber in which their ceremonies would be held to make certain that all was in order. Torches in their brackets sent up tendrils of oily smoke to collect on the damp stones of the ceiling. A raised dais of dark ebony with the delicately carved image of fish had been placed at the far end of the chamber. From there he would address his clergy, and most important, the Holy of Holies was there, set above the dais where all could see it and marvel, for it was the instrument of the death of Jesus Christ at the hands of the Roman legionary Casca Rufio Longinus, who had let out the life blood of the savior.

Walking on bare feet, slowly he approached the spear and knelt before it. Head bowed, he lost himself in prayer, immersing his spirit in righteous hatred for the beast who walked the earth. Crawling forward on his belly, he wormed his way to the spear, tears running down his face in rivers. Ever so slowly, he rose from his stomach to place a shaking finger on the dark stain on the wooden haft, where the blood of Jesus had spilled out on the instrument of his death.

Touching the stain, he felt a cold fire run into his bones. His entire body shook in fevered spasms of ecstatic agony. To be able to actually touch the blood of the living God was a privilege granted only to those most favored. He collapsed to twist spasmodically on the floor, with white foam gathering at the corners of his mouth, flecking his chin, and dropping to the damp stones of the chamber floor. He wept and moaned, crying out in unknown tongues. The acolytes stood in awe of their master on the floor. They tried to let their souls fly with him, envying him his holy experience.

The spell at last eased and then passed. Sobbing, Gregory regained his feet to stumble to his dais and then leaned heavily against it. The time would be soon. He had to get control of his thoughts, though he hated to lose the aura of the touch of God that had overcome him.

The Brethren were entering in two long silent columns. A novice leading each element swung a censure of silver to give off aromatic fumes. All were as he, barefoot in simple robes without adornment, save for a simple silver clasp in the stylized form of the fish, for Jesus was a fisher of men's souls.

Gregory was pleased. Here were the elite of the Brotherhood of the Lamb: the members of the Inner Circle of Thirteen and those of enough merit to be permitted to attend this sacred function.

There was an aura of expectancy running through the kneeling brothers. Without being told, they knew that this was not a normal meeting. Something was going to be said or done that was of special significance.

Gregory cleared his throat. "Welcome, oh ye of the faithful. In the name of God and his Son, I call down the blessings of eternity and paradise upon you. Praise the Lord. Do I hear an amen?''

Two hundred voices responded devoutly: ''Amen. Praise the Lord.''

Gregory nodded his head. ''Then in Jesus's name let us pray. Oh Lord, grant us the strength to do thy holy bidding and prepare the world for thy coming.'' He turned to face the spear. ''In the name of Jesus, let us consecrate ourselves to the day when he shall take us to his bosom and we shall rest forever in the breast of the Lamb and know for eternity the glory of God.'' Gregory turned quickly back to his audience, his voice gaining in intensity and power. He pointed a finger at his flock, crying out, ''Do I hear a hallelujah for the Lord?''

The flock moaned in a rising crescendo, ''Hallelujah! Jesus love us. Praise the Lord!''

Gregory threw back his hood, showing his face for the first time. He had soft, rounded features, the aftereffect of his castration. But the fervor in his eyes was not to be denied. He let the spirit take him. Blood rushed to his face. He pounded his flock with his passion. With tears running from his face, he gave them the message they had come to hear.

''We have failed the Lord. Do you hear me? We have not done our duty, and those before us have likewise broken faith. But we have the chance to redeem ourselves in the sight of God if we have the faith and determination to commit ourselves completely to his holy plan. Are we going to let God down, Brothers?'' he cried.

The members of the Brotherhood beat themselves, renting their chests with their fingernails at the knowledge of their failure, although they didn't know just what that failure was. It was enough that the Elder had said that they had failed God; therefore, they were not in a state of grace.

As one giant sobbing voice, they wept and cried out, ''No! Elder, we shall not fail. We commit ourselves to the holy plan of the Lord and his Son.''

Gregory wept with them. ''Our sin, Brothers, is that the beast has been lost to us for too long. Casca Longinus, that spawn of corruption, has not been found. As you know, he was last seen in the service of Stilicho. Then, after the defeat of Attila, he vanished. He must be found, for he is the road that leads to Jesus, and we have lost him. How can we be with our Lord at the moment of his coming if we don't have the beast to follow? Somewhere he lives, he breathes, and he must be found or we will be condemned to eternal hell and pain for our failure. From this day forth, our most important purpose in life will be to find the beast, wherever he may be hiding. He cannot conceal his curse forever. Somewhere someone will speak of a man who should have died but did not, whose wounds heal miraculously, who bears the scar upon his face and the mark of the Elder Dacort on his right wrist, where his hand was severed from his body, yet it is whole. *Great is the power of God!*" Gregory nearly fainted with passion. "Go ye into the world; search out story, every legend no matter how fantastic. Commit yourselves to this purpose with one will, and we shall prevail.

"The beast shall be found. Let nothing take your minds or efforts away from this purpose. Although it takes a dozen lifetimes, he must be found. When ye go forth from here, find him, find him . . . find him! That we may find the way to Jesus, praise the Lord!"

His message and order were given; now it was time to perform the ritual. A member of the Inner Circle who had reached the time when years had enfeebled his body had begged for permission to be the one who served this day. His request was granted as an acknowledgment of his piety and devotion.

Gregory raised his voice to a clear bell-like tone in joy as he told his Brothers, "Let us do our duty and send the spirit of our Brother to stand beside the throne of God." Pointing his finger at the lucky man, he said, "Rise, Brother, and receive the glory of Jesus!"

The old man before him stripped off his robes to stand clad only in a simple white loincloth. His aged body was shivering with expectation. He had long waited and prayed for this moment.

Gregory knelt in front of the spear and cried out, "Let it be done in the name of Jesus!"

Whips came out from under robes, whips of lead-tipped leather, and heavy ropes with knotted ends. They scourged their brother, reveling in his holy cries of pain as he was permitted to experience all that had happened to Jesus on the day of the crucifixion. Drops of blood fell to the stones, to be walked on by the bare feet of the disciples of Izram.

The old man fell to his knees under the blows, his loose wrinkled skin wincing. He prayed for the strength to reach the final moment. He was dragged to his feet by the loving hands of his brothers. A weight was put on his shoulders. His knees nearly buckled again, but he was aided by their hands even as they beat him.

He was guided along a series of corridors and tunnels through the great drains where the red eyes of rats watched the ceremony from niches in the bricks and wondered whether they would feed this night on fresh meat instead of the offal that came down from the drains to collect in foul streaks of slime along the floors and walls.

The old man moaned as a wreath of thorns was set into the flesh of his forehead. He stumbled forward, one heavy dragging step after another, led by Brothers with torches to light their path. Gregory was in the lead, his head covered by his hood. Hands folded, they chanted, ''Longinus,'' over and over in rhythm with their steps: ''Longinus.''

They entered another large chamber. In the center was a raised set of bricks in which a place had been prepared for the cross their brother carried.

As they neared, the blows on the old man ceased, and they turned the whips on themselves, each striking as hard as he could, letting the ropes and whips cut into their own flesh. They shared their brother's ecstasy as they laid him down and drove spikes into the thin wrists between the large blue veins and then tied his arms to the cross's beams. It took several blows of the mallet to get the spike through the bones of the feet and into the wood block deeply enough to sustain his weight. But it was done, and the Brothers raised the cross to an upright position and then slid it forward until it dropped into the hole prepared for its base. It settled in with a heavy thump and nearly fell over, but it was steadied by eager hands. Then the base was secured by bricks until it stood steady and firm, with the body of their brother hanging from it, his arms stretched out, the shoulders nearly separating from the force of his meager weight.

The old man passed out from the pain and had to be whipped gently to be brought back to consciousness. He had yet to fulfill the full rites of the ceremony; he had to be awake.

Gregory removed his cloak. Under it he wore, as had every Elder on this sacred occasion, the uniform and armor of a legionary of the Jerusalem garrison on that day when their Lord, the Gentle Lamb, had gone to his death.

Gregory signaled an acolyte, and a Roman helmet was

brought for him to complete his costume. Without looking, he stretched out his hand. The spear of Longinus was put into it.

The Brother on the cross tried to focus his eyes through the pain. He had to get out the words or all would be in vain and he would not be granted the mercy of God.

Somewhere he found the strength to croak out, barely audible, the words that Izram had heard Jesus speak nearly five hundred years before from his cross: "My father, why has thou forsaken me?"

The disciples responded with their own anguished cry: "The *spear*, Longinus! Have mercy!"

Gregory decided to rush things a bit before the man on the cross died prematurely. That would have been a bad omen.

The old man continued to speak, gasping out the words as the spear was carefully forced into his side. Not deeply enough to kill immediately—he had to finish playing his part first. Gregory waited until the last words were spoken by the lucky one who had taken Jesus's place on the cross and was to have the honor of experiencing the death of their Lord: "As you are, so you shall remain."

With those last words Gregory shoved the spear home before the old man could die of other causes. He sank the head of the spear in deep, driving it into the lungs. Then he gave another firmer shove, and the point of the spear reached the old man's heart to puncture the muscle and stop its weakening beat. The old man shivered once and died. His mouth full of blood, he hung limp from the cross. The last thought in his mind was how grateful he was not to have died before playing his part. He was truly blessed among men.

Gregory withdrew the spear, leaving an opening through which the old man's thin blood could pour out. It was a woefully thin stream. Gregory made a mental note not to use men of such advanced age again.

The Elder turned to hold the spear above his head, showing his followers the blood on it. He spoke the ancient words that had been passed down from the first Elder to him and were spoken only once a year at this holy conclave:

"Behold the spear of Longinus, the spawn of Satan. Through the blood of the Lamb was he given life . . . life to walk the earth until the master returns. The founder of our order, Izram the Syrian, who came to join the master and become the thirteenth disciple, was at the Mount of Skulls and heard the words of the Lord Jesus that condemned the Roman dog to life. It was Izram who witnessed the blood of the Lamb touching the dog's tongue and thereby transforming him into the undying beast he is now, and Izram who bought the Roman's spear from his comrades after the beast was sentenced to the mines. Izram founded our holy order and gave unto us the keeping of the most holy of relics, the instrument of our Lord's death, the spear of Longinus—Longinus, who must walk the earth until the master comes again. May his every moment be filled with pain, unbearable and prolonged through the centuries; may worms nest in his eyes and rats live in his bowels. Longinus lives through the blood of the Lamb, as we shall live in paradise through the blood of our blessed martyred brother who has become one with the Lord Jesus. Behold the spear of the murderer, the holiest relic in the world, the gateway to heaven.''

Gregory paused to catch his breath. The fervor of the ancient words caught him up as always. His heart was pounding fiercely. Sweat was running down his face, and his eyes bulged in righteous passion. Raising the spear above his head, he sobbed out, ''Brothers, pray with me and curse the name of Longinus, the killer of God!''

He lowered the point of the spear with the thin blood of their sacrifice moving slowly down to the point as the air clotted it. In order, the Brothers crept forward on their knees to touch their tongues against the dark stain that had collected on the point. One after another they tasted the blood of their surrogate lamb and received the holy spirit into themselves. They moved away to fall over, scourging themselves, rolling and crying out the name of the one they hated most in the world: ''Longinus, Longinus.''

The crucifixion was over. The body of their brother was removed from the cross to be washed and cleansed and then wrapped in linen and placed in a tomb prepared in the side of the catacombs and cemented in with bricks.

It was over. Gregory was exhausted. The message had been given, and the ceremony had come off quite well; he was satisfied. He would meet with the others of the Inner Circle the next day to give them their final orders pertaining to the finding of Casca and also to go over their accounts. It seemed as if there never was enough gold to cover all their expenses. But at least many of his followers had positions from which they were able to siphon funds to serve the Brotherhood of the Lamb.

The spear was returned to its case to be put away until the next year, when once again it would serve to remind the faithful of their duties and the honor they had been given in the service of God.

Before the first light of dawn, many of the Brotherhood were already taking varied means of transportation to return to their homelands. A feeling of satisfaction traveled with them, for they knew that they were the chosen few.

In the morning, the members of the Inner Circle attended their Elder at a breakfast held at his villa outside the walls of Constantinople, where they would be assured of absolute privacy.

Gregory was dressed in a loose, flowing, knee-length tunic of pure white wool. The waist was gathered with a single strand of woven gold from which hung the silver image of a fish. His guests were dressed in varied costumes according to their positions in the secular world, though two did wear the robes of Catholic bishops.

Gregory once again thought how wise Izram had been when he had founded the Order of Thirteen. There were thirteen members of the Inner Circle. Each controlled thirteen deacons, who controlled thirteen lay brothers, who controlled thirteen novices or acolytes. Each leader of thirteen knew only the members directly under his control by their true names. In this manner, if their ranks were ever betrayed, the line would cease with their deaths and go no further. Each brother, from the newest novice to the Elder, was firmly committed to die before revealing any information about the order.

As the Elder, Gregory was not only the leader of the Inner Circle but had his own thirteen, who were the swords of their order. From all ranks his thirteen were selected for their strength, intelligence, and courage; of course, they had to be brothers of absolute devotion. They were trained in the matters of security and when needed used their knives or garrottes to enforce discipline or eliminate anyone who interfered with their plans.

At his villa this day, only the members of his Swords of God were in attendance. All other servants and slaves had been sent away. A light breakfast of fresh fruit, cheese, and bread was served. Gregory noticed the way most of his guests sat with their backs away from their chairs. It would be some days before they were able to sleep on their backs without some discomfort.

To these men he repeated his message of the previous evening. Casca must be found, and if they had need of gold, men, or influence, they were not to count the cost or hesitate to call on him for anything. Even a small war was not out of the question if it would help.

During their meal, he passed down what little information he had about the hated one, which was woefully small. He had last been seen, as had been stated, while in the service of Stilicho and had disappeared after the withdrawal of Attila and his Huns from Italy. There had been an unconfirmed report that he had been seen at a tavern near the foothills of the Julian Alps, where one of their lay brothers was master. But that had been long ago. The beast could be anywhere, but he would show up again. He always did.

CHAPTER TWO

The Warrior

Wearily, the warrior trudged up the trail past a grove of pines. The shield on his back rubbed a sore spot on his shoulder where the strap cut into his flesh. Eyes down on the pine needle-covered deer trail, he moved forward with heavy shuffling steps. The spear in his right hand pointed its steel head down in front of him in the manner in which a blind man uses his staff to search his sightless way through the Stygian darkness of his existence.

But this man was not blind, though there had been many times when he wished that he'd had no eyes to see the horrors of his existence. His appearance would give any watcher hesitation: the worn battered jacket of iron scales under his fur robe, the steel helmet resting low over his forehead, the nose guard raised, but most of all, the aura of terrible bloody death that was in the gray-blue eyes.

Those eyes had seen the rise and fall of many nations, emperors and kings, gods and devils. He was a man who had been both god and demon, soldier and slave. He was Casca Longinus, the damned. The curse of Jesus the Nazarene was ever with him since the moment when his pilum had pierced the side of the one they had called the messiah over four hundred years before.

"Soldier," Jesus had said, "you are content with what you are, then that you shall remain until we meet again."

The words had meant nothing to him then as the blood of the Jew rushed out to cover his spear and his hand where he touched it to his lips unthinkingly and thereby took the blood of Jesus into his own body. He was damned. Damned! Damned to a life of eternal conflict and suffering. Condemned to live until the second coming of Jesus. Condemned to walk the earth without ever knowing peace or even the comfort of having his own family, for he knew that his blood was sick and that the seed of his body would never grow in the womb of a mortal woman.

He had known love, but always it had been taken from him by the insidious passage of time. He couldn't stay with a woman who would one day question him as to why his face didn't show the normal ravages of time or why disease never stayed in his body or why wounds healed that should have killed him.

The day always came when once more he would put his shield on his back, his sword in its scabbard, and move on to the next battle: endless battles, screaming faces, and rivers of blood to feed the ambitions of those who would be kings. Even in this he had no choice, for Jesus had said, "As you are, so you shall remain." He was a soldier of the legions then, and a soldier he would remain. He was the eternal mercenary.

Below, in the warmer lands of Italy, he had left behind battlefields littered with the thousands of corpses that had fallen in battle against Attila and his Huns. Even worse were those who had died from the fevered touch of war's handmaiden, plague.

His body was thick and heavily muscled, the body of a man born to fight. Under the robe and armor were scars to attest his trials. Thick-fingered hands that could barely handle a writing quill could move a spear or sword with the ease of a master painter. He was death's artist, who painted on fate's canvas from a palette of fire and blood, leaving his lifeless works behind on his long journey to eternity.

A whipping branch struck him across the face, causing his eyes to water and bringing him back to reality. Cursing, he wiped the tears from his eyes with the back of his left hand and moved up the mountain trail. A rushing sound ahead of him brought his spear up to the ready position. He moved off the trail, concealing himself behind a tree. The sound came closer. Someone was running. A figure broke through the brush to his front and fell to the ground a few feet from where he stood.

A woman lay on her knees, huddled over. Wracking sobs came from her in short gasping barks as she struggled to get her breath. She was holding something to her chest. From where he stood, it looked like a bundle of rags.

Casca stepped back onto the trail, and his shadow fell across the woman. She raised red-rimmed panicked eyes and screamed, holding the bundle to her breast. Whimpering in terror, she backed away on her knees until her back came against the rough bark of tree and she could go no farther. As she moved, Casca saw that the bundle she held was not a pack of rags but a child, a baby of no more than a year. He also knew that the baby was dead.

As the woman cringed in terror, part of the dingy blanket around her child fell away, and he saw the reason for the child's death. It had been stabbed repeatedly. The sight of those ugly wounds on the young flesh set in his brain like acid. This was the worst part of his curse, to have to witness the endless slaughter of innocents.

He knelt down in front of the woman, speaking slowly and carefully, his voice gentle but firm. "Where are those that did this thing?" He didn't ask who had done it. That made no difference.

He moved the thin blanket back up to cover the child's ugly wounds. This act served to stop the woman's screams. Again he repeated, "Where are those that did this thing?"

The woman pointed back up the trail with a dirty finger on which the blood had not yet clotted, and by this Casca knew that they were near.

He rose from his knees, unslung his shield, and put it on his left arm. Then he lowered the nasal guard of his helmet. Looking down on the poor woman and her child, he spoke gently: "Your babe is dead. I cannot help him, but I can see that those who would do a thing like this know pain. Bury your child, woman, but know that his death will be paid for."

Casca turned from her and moved along the trail. Stretching his legs out, with the spear held in front of him, he half ran through the woods. He reached the treeline in less than five minutes and saw across an open field of mountain grass the upright logs that served as a palisade for the small village of thatch-roofed huts and shacks.

From where he was, he could tell that the puny barrier was better suited for keeping livestock in than raiders out. He couldn't see any sign of men on the wall, and so he struck out straight for the wall. Moving up against the logs, he caught his breath and listened. Inside, he could hear the mixed cries of pain and pleasure. The cries were few, and so he figured that there couldn't be too many inside. Most of the villages in this region had fewer than a hundred people, and this one looked to be a bit smaller than that.

He worked his way around to the right of the wall until he could see the gate. It was open, which he expected, but if it hadn't been, it still would not have been any problem to get over the top of the logs.

Slipping inside, he stayed close to the walls of the huts and in the shadows. He passed the bodies of several men, women, and a few children of varying ages who had been put to the sword. One of the men was still breathing, but Casca didn't have time to see whether he could do anything for him.

He saw two warriors guarding a longhouse, probably the one bachelor males lived in. Both were armed with spears and swords. What tribe they were from he couldn't tell. From their coloring they looked to be Germans or perhaps Goths: fair-sized, full-bearded, rough-looking specimens who were badly in need of bathing.

From inside the longhouse he could hear voices, some of which were crying. The surviving villagers were obviously being kept in there. Like most longhouses, there was only one entrance and exit; therefore, two men could easily keep those inside under control, for the entrance was such that people could enter or leave it only one at a time on hands and knees.

Casca unslung the shield from his shoulder and put it on his left arm. It was of the common round type, of ox skin with an iron boss in the center and studs of brass spotted over the rest of the hide. Moving away from the longhouse, he looked for the rest of the raiders. It was easy to find them. The village was not large, and the sounds of laughter led him to where the other invaders were taking their pleasure with the women of the village.

A rape was in progress. One of the raiders had thrown a woman to the earth and then lay on top of her, forcing her legs apart as he dropped his leather breeches over his knees. There were eight women, of whom three hadn't reached the twelfth year, but then, barbarians were never particular. He remembered times when toothless crones were as eagerly raped as if they had been young, full-bodied women.

He didn't choose to interrupt them at their pleasures at this time. There might more than the four men taking turns with their captives. They would have to wait a few minutes until he circled the village to make sure of their numbers.

This was done quickly. He found only two others at different spots, searching through the huts for anything of value. These died quickly and silently when his fingers knotted around their throats to squeeze the life from them.

Once he was sure that there were no more, Casca returned to where the two warriors were guarding the longhouse. It was wisest to take out the small numbers first before tackling the larger group.

There was a space of about fifty feet separating him from the two guards when he looked around the corner of the hut. He would have to be patient. The women should keep the others occupied long enough for him to finish here.

The two guards laughed and joked over their good fortune in finding this place where they would winter; it was fully supplied with food and women to keep them warm during the icy nights.

Casca set his shield down, loosened his sword in its scabbard, and took a different grip on his spear. Waiting until the two men were lined up the way he wanted them, he sucked in a deep breath and ran three long steps toward them, twisting his body to put the full force of his arm and his motion behind the cast. The spear streaked straight for the two men.

One of the guards had his back to the longhouse, facing his comrade, whose back was to Casca. He just had time to see Casca over his comrade's shoulder before the spear entered the latter's back with such force that two feet of it exited through the man's stomach with enough power left to sink a foot into his own soft belly. As Casca threw, he kept on running. He was on them nearly as quickly as the spear. A quick swipe with his sword and he cut a throat, opening up the esophagus of the man whose back had been to the longhouse, stopping a scream that had only reached the back of his throat before Casca let it hiss out with the last of the air in the warrior's lungs.

Casca called softly inside the low opening of the longhouse until a grizzled gray head appeared. Hogar, the elder of the village, looked with surprise and confusion at the two dead warriors and then at the face of the scarred man speaking to him.

"How many do you have in there?" The scar-faced speaker pointed back the way Hogar had come.

"Forty-two, master, all that are left of us. Mostly women or children and four grown men who were saved to be sold at the slave markets in the south."

Casca nodded. "Take them and get out of here. Head for the

woods until I signal you to come back.''

The elder tried to persuade Casca to let him and the other men aid in killing the last of the raiders. Casca shook his shaggy head. "You would just get in the way. You're not warriors, and even if you outnumbered them, they would still slaughter you like sheep. Also, I would have to watch out for you, and that would make me vulnerable. Do as I say. It won't take long.'' He left, not waiting for Hogar to agree to his orders. He knew that they would obey.

He picked up the two spears of the men he had just killed, tucked them under his arm, retrieved his shield, and went to where the others were still involved with their women captives.

A new one had been selected for their pleasure. A girl whose breasts had not yet grown past the budding stage was being held down for one of the raiders to grunt over, thrusting his hips forward, ignoring her cries and cursing her for being too tight. He stopped her screams by giving her a solid blow on the temple. Casca could hear the skull crack from his position behind a storeroom. The raider did not care that he was on a dead girl. He continued his grunting over her limp body, laughing at how she had finally stopped whining.

Casca moved until he was behind the warriors. Then he picked his first target, carefully selecting the toughest-looking of the men for his first cast. The warriors were overconfident. They had laid their heavy shields down and were leaning on their spears, making witty observations about their comrade's performance, saying, "If you'll ride a dead girl, why not a dead horse?''

He drew back over his shoulder and let fly. The spear entered the space separating the shoulder blades, severing the spinal column and passing through the heart, splitting the great muscle open. The man was dead before he hit the ground. Without pause, Casca threw once more. This time he caught a man in the groin and cursed himself for hitting too low.

The last two tried to get organized, but the one on top of the dead girl found his breeches snarled up in her legs and couldn't get to his feet. Casca hit the remaining standing warrior straight on with a shield smash that pounded him to the earth and then a straight thrust with the point of his long sword into the eye socket. The sword stuck in the bone. He didn't want to take time to twist it out, and so he left it in the eye and rushed on to the remaining man, who was still trying to get his pants untangled from the thin legs of the girl he had killed.

Casca dropped his shield to pick up one of the spears that had fallen to the ground. He butt stroked the rapist across the face, smashing his nose and knocking him back to the ground. Casca grabbed the man by his tangled hair and jerked him back to his knees. From his blubbering speech, Casca figured that he was a Gepid, a member of the tribes who were once the most devoted allies of the Huns and equally savage. The warrior begged for his life, promising to be Casca's slave for eternity.

"No! I don't think eternity should have to wait that long for one such as you. You like to stick things into young girls. Perhaps you should know what that feels like."

Casca gave him a solid smash in the spine with his knee. As the man's back arched in pain, he grasped his spear with both hands and struck down, pushing the head of the spear into the thin skin between the collarbone and shoulder. Leaning on the haft, Casca put all his weight behind the thrust, forcing the point deeper into the kneeling man. The cold point sliced through lungs and intestines until it found the only exit available. Still Casca leaned on the handle. Forcing the point deep into the earth, he pinned the squirming Gepid to the ground.

It was done. He told the remaining women to go outside the compound and call in the rest of the villagers. They did as he ordered. While they were gone, he untangled the dead child's legs from the breeches of the Gepid. He regretted that he hadn't gotten to them sooner. He knew that his decision to go after the other raiders first was the right one, but it didn't make the brutal death of this child any easier to accept.

The people of the village crowded around Casca, wanting to touch him in gratitude but afraid to lay hands on him. What if he was just going to take the place of those he had killed?

They had no reason to worry. Casca wanted nothing from them. The passion was gone from his spirit, and this day's work had done nothing to make him feel any better. Reluctantly, he accepted their offer of hospitality and stayed the night, sleeping in a hut whose owners had been killed by the raiders.

The food brought to him was tasteless in his mouth, as though he were eating ashes. He even sent away the woman who came to him in the night and slid under his blanket. He wanted nothing from anyone.

When the woman reported back to Hogar the results of her effort, the old man shook his head in wonder. Surely this man was not like any he had seen before.

When Casca had stripped to wash the blood from himself, Hogar had seen the scars on his body. To his old mind returned many of the legends of his childhood, when he had believed in the stories of the immortals and of those who were half gods.

There was a power to this man with the scarred hands and twisted muscles that worked under his hide. The old man had been a warrior in his youth and had seen many wounds inflicted in battle. He knew that several wounds on the bathing warrior should have killed the man. Had a godling come to save them?

Why else would the warrior refuse what they had offered him? Even their most beautiful woman? But then, what can mere mortals offer that the gods don't already have? Hogar shook his gray head in confusion. It was too much for him to reason out. He knew only that there was no evil in the man who slept in the hut, his sword by his hand.

To Hogar's simple mind, Casca was the representation of Tyr or Wodan, the ancient gods of war of the barbarians. He couldn't be a god of the Romans. He had seen statues of them when young, and they never had bodies like Casca's or carried the scars of a hundred battles. No! He was not a god of the Romans; he wasn't pretty enough for that. But he was still something that was outside the old man's experience.

Casca rose well before first light and left the village, striking straight out toward the high peaks that glistened in the clear, crisp night sky. He didn't try to plan his steps but just let them take him where they wanted to go. And that was up. Up high, past the line where trees could live. Up past where man could exist. Up to the clean mountains, where the stench of death was only a dim breath from the lands below.

It felt good to feel the snow beneath him as he reached the level where early snows had already come to the mountains and soon would work their way down to the green valleys. Ahead of him, he knew that it would be even deeper.

Numbness reached up to Casca's thighs as he forced his way through the growing drifts of white crystals. His lungs ached from the thin air as he stopped to try to catch his breath. Everything around him was a shifting sea of snow. Breath came in short gasps of mist from his open mouth.

Ice tears tried to force his reddened lids together. He rubbed away the rime with the back of a scarred hand. Raising his head, he saw through the swirling clouds the heaven-reaching peaks of the high Alps.

To the south below, in the still, warm valleys of Italy, new masters ruled. The empire was finally destroyed. He knew that she would not rise again. Gaiseric, the Vandal king, had looted Rome for the third time, a systematic sacking of the city that had once and for all broken any remnants of pride or spirit that remained in the hearts of the people.

Only the Eastern Empire remained as a force to be reckoned with, and he knew that it was only a matter of time before the barbarians on her borders would drag down the walls of Constantinople as well.

Casca would have laughed if his face hadn't been so numb from the cold. A matter of time. Gods, he was tired of it all. The last few months since the death of Attila had not eased anything for him. They had brought only one struggle after another that had finally driven him to this desolate valley of ice, where he couldn't see any sign of the works or slaughter of man.

He moved on, his feet growing heavier with each step as his booted feet punched holes in the crisp crust of the drifts. Behind him, his trail was erased in a matter of minutes by the wind. He wished that he could be erased as easily.

He remembered the dream of Alaric the Ostrogoth, how he wanted to rebuild the empire by infusing the vitality of his race with the culture of Rome. Perhaps it would work, perhaps not. Casca was so tired that he really didn't care who ruled the world or in what name.

Casca's lungs ached from his exertions. Reaching the base of the peak, he stood in a sheltered place between a schism of granite that had been split open by the expansion of drops of water that had collected in a thousand tiny crevices. Finally, during some unknown epoch, the water had been frozen hard enough to expand a thousandth of an inch and then hundreds of times more over the next ten thousand years, repeating the process, each time forcing the granite farther apart until the ice won and the tons of rock gave up, to burst open.

Looking back over the way he had come, in the valley below, he could see the face of a glacier, blue lights bouncing from its surface as the wind eased and then finally ceased, leaving the countryside clear to view: clean, cold, and pure.

Without knowing why, he began to climb the mountain, fol-

lowing a narrow trail for five thousand feet. Then, where it
ended, he saw a small cave facing out over the shining valleys
below. Here the wind had swept away most of the snow. The
chill of the thin air cut like a dagger, but he didn't care; it meant
nothing. In a strange way it felt good.

He sat down a few feet from the entrance, his legs crossed,
holding his sword in his hand, with the point of the scabbard between his legs. For some reason he put on his helmet, the iron
nasal guard down, his shield on his back, the spear by his right
thigh. The thick black bearskin was draped over his shoulders as
he sat waiting for something. But he was content. There was a
peacefulness to the cold. His lungs had quit aching for breath as
he stared out over the ice fields below, waiting, waiting, weary.

Outside of the cave the valleys and peaks of ice cast rainbows
over the horizon. He was so tired. As the blood in his veins began to thicken, he started to feel warmer, comfortable, alone in
his granite tower. He leaned his head against the pommel of his
sword, letting the winter sink deep into his soul, taking him
away. His eyes couldn't move; tears had frozen them open. But
he felt no pain. His body was a distant thing that he was only
vaguely aware of.

His thoughts came slowly as the feeling drained from him,
beginning in his legs and then rising slowly up into his abdomen
till he could barely sense a warm chill touching his heart and
slowing it down.

He sat, sword in his hands, head leaning against his weapon.
His unmoving eyes saw nothing as he let the cold claim him.
Before it took him completely, his distant mind whispered to
him a piece of verse he heard a hundred years before:

> *Endlessly weary,*
> *the Silent Sentinel*
> *guards the Tower of Darkness.*
> *Endlessly, endlessly weary.*

The warrior slept, eyes open to the winds, not caring, not
knowing when his mind ceased to be aware of anything, anyone, even himself. Not knowing or caring about the ice that
gradually encrusted his body or the paleness of his hands and
face that could no longer move or wished to.

The warrior, with his weapons, slept the long sleep of the ice
mountains in his own tower of white darkness.

It was the next spring when the villager found him in the cave. All color was gone from his face, and his hands still grasped the sword between his legs. His eyes were open, sightlessly watching the valley below. Even though the glaciers beneath him were starting to give off streams of clear melted ice—water to flow to the rivers and thence to the distant seas—there in the heights it would always be winter for the sleeping warrior.

The shepherd stood in superstitious awe of the frozen man. Making a sign to ward off evil, he ran back to his village as fast as his legs could carry him, rushing in to breathlessly call the people to come and witness what he had seen. The warrior had not left them; he was still there: above them, waiting, watching over them.

Hogar the elder questioned the shepherd, shaking his gray head in confusion and wonder, for the man swore that the warrior was not dead. He had seen many who had frozen to death in the mountains, but there was a difference to this man of the sword. He couldn't put the difference into words, but if they would just come see for themselves, they would know that he spoke the truth.

In the morning Hogar took two of his men and a woman with him, the one whose murdered child Casca had avenged. Together they made the long climb up the narrow twisting trail, far past the line where trees grew and only a few stubborn bushes and gray lichens could survive. When they reached the cave, Hogar stopped, his heart pounding more in anticipation of what he might find than it had from the climb. Summoning up his courage, he looked inside the cave. It was true!

The warrior was there, legs crossed in front of him, holding his weapons, staring with unblinking ice-gray eyes. He knelt in front of the warrior as the others crowded behind him.

There was something different about him, a feeling that he was not dead, though he certainly looked to be. No man could survive a winter in the heights alone, without food or warm shelter, yet there was no sign that a fire had ever been made here. But there was still something about the warrior that just wasn't right. Timidly, Hogar reached out a hand to touch the cheek of the man who had saved them from the bandits.

He jerked his hand back as if it had been burned. The skin should have been hard as a rock, yet there was an odd suppleness to it in spite of the chill that lay behind the gray unmoving flesh.

CHAPTER THREE

Ireina

Beneath the sleeper, the world turned as always. Powers rose and fell. Babies were born, to grow until they had their own children and then die. Wars came, famines struck, and nothing really changed except the names. Man was as he always had been and always would be, driven by the same fears and motivations that had plagued him since the first cell had crawled out of the primal slime of creation to eventually stand erect and leave the shelter of the cave.

None of this mattered to the sleeper, for he considered his long sleep as an escape for a time from the conflict of life.

Only the boundaries of nations changed. As new masters rose and fell in the year 454, the Gepids, under the command of Arderic, turned on their Hunnish overlords and destroyed them in a great battle at the Nedao. The surviving Huns retreated back to the steppes of central Asia, to the shores of the Sea of Azov, pushing the last survivors of the glory of Ermanrich's Ostrogoths into a small pocket of the Crimea.

By *A.D.* 455, after the conquest of Africa by the Vandal King Gaiseric, the Mediterranean was a German lake. Gaiseric built a great fleet and claimed the Balearics, Corsica, Sardinia, and the western end of Sicily. His wild raiders struck east and west at will and sacked Rome much more thoroughly than it had been pillaged when the Goths of Alaric rode through the gates.

By 470, the final disintegration of the Western Empire was complete. The Visigoths expanded to the Loire and Rhone rivers in Gaul and then conquered Spain except for those portions already held by their cousins, the Suevii, and small inaccessible and hostile regions populated by the fierce tribes of the Basques.

The names of many tribes disappeared as they were either totally eliminated or absorbed into larger ones, such as the Burgundians, who now ruled from the Alps to the Mediterranean, as the Franks and Alemanni slowly spread out from their borders.

Italy was in the hands of Odoacer, a barbarian general who finally dispensed with the services of even a puppet emperor and took all power to himself. He did acknowledge the suzerainty of the Eastern emperor, but only with the proviso that no attempt be made to enforce his fealty. Odoacer destroyed the fierce Rugians so completely when they attempted to cross the Danube into what was now his land that they vanished as people from history.

The last province where a Roman emperor ruled in the west was Dalmatia, and after the death of the last of the ''Roman emperors,'' Romulus Caesar, he annexed that province and proclaimed himself King of Italy, only in 489 to fall to treachery at the hands of Theodoric the Ostrogoth after four years of hardfought battles.

Italy changed masters as other men change wives. All of the proud empire of the Caesars, from Europe to Africa, was now in the hands of the German tribes, and barbarians sat on the eagle throne of Rome.

All this took place as the warrior slept the long sleep, not noticing the offerings that were placed before him by the villagers. His eyes of ice never saw the flowers set before him that quickly withered into brown dried husks that blew away with the winds or tasted the food that was set before him by the villagers. The warrior had no need of these things, for he knew neither hunger nor thirst.

For the first hundred years, the people of the village came to his cave at regular intervals to place their offerings, but eventually the worshipers found new interests and the offerings became fewer with each passing season until at last years would pass before anyone would take the effort to climb to his granite nest. It was too much trouble.

There were a few among the older people who still told of how he had come to their valley and saved them. By the cooking fires, the children would sit at their feet at night as they told of the warrior and how he had gone to the mountain so that he could always watch over them. If the day came when he was needed again, he would awaken and come down from the gale-swept peaks to do battle against their enemies.

The children would listen with wide eyes at the story, and once in a while one of them would gather his courage to climb the mountain and see whether the warrior was really there.

They would return from their adventure, breathless with excitement and fear at their own daring, to tell the others that the warrior was there. He was still sitting holding his sword, eyes open, his face as gray as the stones around him, ice crystals forming diamonds in his hair, covering his fur robe in a thin crust of rime.

In time, as they grew older, they no longer believed in the legend, for that is what it had become by then. The warrior was just a man who had frozen to death. That and no more, though several times a young man found enough courage to try to take the sword from the hand of the warrior, for swords such as he held were of great value. Such a weapon could buy a man enough cattle to start his own herd.

But always, when they reached out to force the stiff white fingers from around the blade, they stopped. There was something that came over them, a nameless dread that said, "Leave this alone," when they touched the cold scarred hands. The eyes of the warrior watched them, unmoving, but they seemed somehow aware. No one ever succeeded in taking the blade from its master's grasp or even spoke of the attempt to do so.

The warrior was left alone in his tower.

Ireina followed the thin trail up to the heights. She'd sneaked away from her older brother, who was watching their small flock of goats and sheep below. The story of the warrior, as told her by her great-grandmother, filled her with too much childish curiosity to resist going to see for herself.

Even though she had been born in the highlands, her heart pounded under her ten-year-old rib cage as her lungs labored under the thin air. The wind whipped her long strands of silver hair about her head and face under the garland of spring flowers she'd woven.

The journey was taking longer than she had thought it would, and she knew that she would be in trouble when she got back to her brother—but she had to go. She turned a corner around a jagged edge of granite, and there was the cave.

Hesitant now at her own daring, she walked slowly forward, shivering under her thin tunic. A patch of ice in the shade of the monolith nearly caused her to slip and fall. If she had, it would have certainly killed her, for the next stop was over five hundred feet straight down.

Shadows were on the face of the entrance to the cave as she crept slowly forward. Finally, she could see a dim figure near the mouth. For a moment she thought it was just a strangely shaped boulder. Then, as she neared, she saw the man.

Moving in to see him better, she squatted on her thin haunches directly in front of him, not moving until her eyes adjusted from the glare outside to the darker shadows in the cave. The man's face came into full vision. She caught her breath. He looked dead, yet there was something that said he was not. She knew that most of her people believed him to just be a frozen man, but she knew different. Slowly she moved closer to him, careful not to touch the sword in his scarred hand. Moving a little to his side, she looked him over from all angles.

The face was not cruel—hard, yes, but not cruel. In her child's heart she saw a terrible sadness in the set of the mouth, a great weariness in the manner in which the broad shoulders sloped under the frozen robe. She moved her face closer to his, nearly touching him. She looked into the eyes, eyes that never blinked, yet she felt that they knew she was there.

A strange desire came over her; she set her young lips to the pale ones of the warrior, expecting to feel stiff, ice-frozen flesh. She jerked back when the flesh yielded under her lips. His lips were cold, but she knew that there was life behind them. She became frightened of her boldness and her thoughts. Removing the garland of flowers from her hair, she set them in the lap of the warrior and turned to race back down the mountain as fast as her legs would take her.

That night she didn't think of the slap her brother had given her for going off. Instead, her mind was filled with the face of the man in the cave, and she dreamed childish dreams of how one day he would awaken to take her from the mountain down into the warm lands. He was hers.

As she grew, so did her fantasies about Casca. He represented all the things she dreamed of: a sleeping noble who would make her his bride and come to her rescue when danger threatened.

Keeping the secret to herself, she made regular trips to the cave, spending hours there talking to the man, not minding that he didn't answer. She told him all her secret dreams and thought that she saw his head nod in understanding or his mouth twist just a bit in a tiny smile.

Each time before she left, she would kiss the gray lips and tell him to rest well till she came again. The young men of the village who courted her found themselves rejected firmly. No matter what they offered, she would not lay down with them or take one to mate, even though she had now reached the sixteenth year of her life and was as beautiful and wild as the mountains of her home.

Her father shook his head in resignation that his daughter was a bit strange, but he hoped that she would grow out of it and take a mate soon. But she never even entertained the thought of taking one of the men of the mountains to wed. She had her lover high in the mountains; he waited, and so did she. One day he would come for her, and she would be there.

Ireina's high valley was seldom visited by the new masters, for it was off the beaten paths and had little to offer in the way of riches. Occasionally a rider came to tell them that they were to pay tribute in the amount of a few sheep or cattle, either to the Burgundians or to the Ostrogoths, whichever was most in power at that moment. Sometimes they had to pay both, for they sat near an undefined border between the two states. The Ostrogoths controlled Italy proper and were the stronger, but they had other richer regions to tax and were seldom hard pressed enough to send warriors into this sparsely populated region for the sake of few sheep or cows. They only came in the summer months, when the passes were clear of ice and snow.

Their worst fears were about the bands of raiders and bandits who wandered the mountains, taking refuge from the warriors of the new masters. These were not so choosy. All knew that it was only a matter of time before they showed up again, though now it had been two full generations since a band of brigands had last entered their valley. That had not been too difficult an ordeal. A patrol of Burgundians was hot on their trail, and the brigands moved off after killing a few villagers and taking what little they had in the way of movable goods. Their loot consisted of less than ten silver coins and a few pots of copper. They took nothing else—even slaves would have slowed them down—as they were short of horses.

Ireina prayed for her sleeping lover to awaken, but he didn't.

The old ones of the village said that he would not come down until the village was in desperate danger. Ireina was torn between hoping for disaster to strike and fear that it would.

It was the fall of her twentieth year when what they'd dreaded came to pass. A band of fifty warriors from different tribes rode into her valley and made themselves master there. This time there would be no pursuit, for the first snows were already beginning to close up the narrow passes and trails. There could be no aid until the spring thaw.

The village had increased in size but still numbered no more than a hundred males, of whom fewer than twenty were of an age to fight.

The bandits rode in nearly unopposed. Several young men attempted to resist but were quickly cut down. The leader of the bandits was named Herac, a tall, darkly handsome man with a shaven face who was half Greek and half Goth. He affected cleaner habits than his cohorts but was not lacking in their greed and cruelty.

As the leader, he had first choice among the women, and he picked Ireina. She was led to him where he had set up headquarters in the longhouse for bachelor males. It was the largest building in the village.

She closed her eyes and her mind to what happened to her as he forced himself into her body, his rough hands bruising her breasts, whipping her to try to get some response. She lay still, saying nothing, doing nothing, as he performed one vile exercise after another on her. She took her mind away from what was happening to her body, giving Herac, who considered himself quite a lover, no satisfaction. Finally he beat her and threw her out of the longhouse, cursing her for being a stupid cow who couldn't please a real man.

That night the first heavy snow came falling in a windless sky to cover the earth and fields. The old women treated her wounds, washing away the blood from her thighs. When they at last left her alone, she dressed, ignoring the pain, took food and a warm robe, wrapped her legs in wool breeches, and climbed out over the stockade wall. She knew where she had to go.

Her trail was covered in a matter of minutes as the snow continued to fall in fat, gentle flakes.

It was dawn when she reached the opening to the cave where the warrior slept. Wrapping herself in her robe, she lay down beside him.

The cold of dawn woke her, her body aching and her legs cramped under her. The temperature had dropped to far past the point of freezing. Sitting up next to Casca, she rubbed the pain from her legs, trying to get the circulation started again. She had to stay warm, or she would join her sleeping lover. The thought appealed to her: to sit beside him through eternity, never knowing pain or hunger, to be always young.

The chill set in deeply. Her lips turned blue and her limbs numb; she knew what she had to do. Wrapping her robe closer to her body, she left the cave and went back down the trail for two thousand feet until she reached the treeline. She gathered fallen branches from under the snow and hauled them back to the cave. Three time she made the trip, ignoring the pain of her wounds and the cramping in her loins and stomach.

Once she started moving, the cold wasn't so bad, but she knew that if she stopped, she would never rise again. At last she had the final load and sat, breasts heaving, in the cave as the sightless eyes of Casca looked over the emptiness of the new winter.

Finding rocks in the rear of the cave, she piled them as high as they would go in the entrance. Hesitantly, she managed to take the stiff frozen bearskin from around Casca's shoulders and use it to plug the small opening that remained.

That accomplished, she took flint, steel, and lint from her pouch to start a small fire. Sparingly, she fed the tiny flame, knowing that it would not take much to warm up the small confines of her shelter. She didn't want to have to make the journey back down the mountain for more wood any sooner than necessary.

Slowly, the cave began to warm up for the first time since it had been formed millennia before. It passed the freezing point a few degrees and then a few more.

Ice began to melt in Casca's beard, and melted frost ran in tears down his unmoving cheeks to lie in tiny puddles on the stone floor.

Ireina slept deeply from her exertions. The heat built rapidly in the small confines of their shelter and lulled her into deep slumber, but another was beginning to awake.

With the increase in temperature, the thick sluggish blood in Casca's body began to flow a tiny bit easier through arteries and veins that were regaining some of their flexibility.

His heart warmed under the flow of blood, giving a slightly

stronger beat and then another, gradually picking up the tempo of true life. With the increase of his heartbeat, blood was forced down into the lower regions of his body where it had been drawn away to feed the body cavity and heart when first he had sat down to freeze.

His lungs gave a jerking labored movement as they sucked in a large quantity of the warming air involuntarily. The intake of oxygen fed the blood cells, sending a burst of sensation down into his extremities. The thick fluid behind the gray eyes thawed as thousands of small vessels and capillaries opened to welcome the unfamiliar surge of warmth. One eye blinked and then the other. His face began to gather spots of color around the cheekbones. His lips lost their gray paleness, and with the return of blood came pain.

His entire system came to life in one spasmodic effort. It was too much too soon for organs and vessels that had shrunk from the century he had slept, each year using up a tiny bit of their remaining moisture.

His mouth opened, though his mind had not yet awakened, and a scream came forth. He was on fire, the same pain a man feels who has had frostbite and then warms the frozen limb too rapidly.

The guttural screams woke Ireina in a panic. Had the brigands followed her?

When her eyes focused, she saw the source of the cry of anguish. The warrior's mouth was open, filling his lungs again and again to let out his cry of torment as the warmth of his blood thawed the cells of his body.

His sword dropped from stiff fingers, his back arched, and for the first time in over a hundred years he straightened out his legs and screamed once more. Then he fell onto his back unconscious, letting his system complete its job of restoring him to humanity.

Ireina watched in shock as the warrior went through his agony. She wasn't frightened, only stunned by his resurrection.

Then it came to her. All that she had prayed for had come to pass. Her childhood dreams were becoming reality. The sentinel was awakening, and he would protect her and punish those in the valley below.

The training of her youth in the cold of the mountains took

over. She knew instinctively what was causing part of the warrior's pain, and she began to treat him as she would one who had spent the night in a snowdrift.

She covered his body with her own robe, not trying to remove the rusty armor from his body. Then she tugged at him to pull him farther inside. She thought that he would have weighed more, not knowing that the gradual loss of fluid in his cells had wasted away thirty pounds. From her sack, she removed a small copper pot. Moving Casca's bear robe aside, she scooped snow from outside to fill the pot, and then she set the pot over the small flame.

Into the pot she put shaved strands of dried meat to simmer along with herbs and a small amount of precious salt. At this altitude, even though the mixture boiled fiercely, she knew that it was just past being lukewarm. But that was well enough. Something too hot might hurt her patient, who was silent now, his breathing a bit easier, though she knew from the expression on his unconscious face that he was still in great pain. His legs and arms trembled and twitched spasmodically, his hands opening and closing of their own accord as his body shook.

She removed his helmet, noting the deep lines sunk into his forehead where the steel brim had rested, its weight pressing ever deeper until it almost reached the bone of the skull. A strip of loose skin came away from his nose as she pulled the cold steel from his face.

Touching his skin, she was surprised to feel how dry it was. There was no suppleness to the tissue. She pinched the back of his hand, pulling the skin up only to to see it remain there, not going back to its original position. She knew from the old women that that was a sure sign of lack of fluids. Gently, she moistened her fingers in the pot and patted the broth onto his lips, careful not to crack them.

The fluid sank into the parched lips until she was able carefully to pry them back a bit and slip half a wooden spoonful into his mouth. Then she waited a moment before giving him another. The broth was absorbed into the dried membranes of his mouth, bringing flexibility back to the gums that had pulled partially away from the teeth.

His system welcomed the new flow of energy, attacking the broth greedily as she was able to spoon the contents of the pot faster into him. At last a spoonful made it all the way into his stomach, where it started the flow of digestive juices that had long lay dormant.

She then set about removing his armor and clothes, her fingers stumbling over the unfamiliar straps and buckles that held it to him. Once she had managed to free him of that encumbrance and had set it aside by his shield, sword, and spear, it was easy to get the rest of his clothes off. She sucked in her breath at the sight of his body: not at his nakedness but at the wounds that had been inflicted on him.

She refilled the pot and set it to warm the snow; then she tore a piece of rag from her clothes and soaked it in the warm water and began to wash his body. He was like a piece of sun-dried parchment. The fluid on the rag never left a wet mark on his skin as his pores soaked it all in to feed his starving tissues. She saw this and, not understanding the reason, knew what she had to do. Not dipping this time, she poured the water into her hand and began to rub. She refilled the pot seven times before she saw a glow and suppleness return to the flesh. She never noticed that the winter sun had set as she labored over her man, for that's what he was to her mind. Had she not brought him back to life?

All that night she fed and bathed him in turn. To her, it was a miracle the way his features changed. He was still thin, but there was life behind the sleeping, twitching lids. She wondered whether he dreamed and, if so, of what.

At last, too weary to continue, she lay down under the robes with Casca after first putting a few more twigs on their fire. She snuggled close to his naked body. Putting her head on his shoulder, she slept content. Sometimes dreams do come true, and now all would be well.

The unconscious agony of his rebirth passed. Casca slowly felt his eyes open, burning slightly, sticky and heavy. The lids seemed to have weights holding them shut. As of yet, his body was a distant foreign thing, and there was pressure on his body and chest. He moved his head to see what it was.

His eyes were still fogged. All he could make out was a blurred halo of silver lying in waves around a face. Blinking, he tried to focus. Slowly the face came into view. He felt like he was having some kind of strange dream, where the taste of it stays with you long after you awake and it takes some time before you accept the fact that it all happened in your sleep.

Ireina moaned softly and shifted her body closer to him. The warm feel of her full breasts next to his bare chest and the firm leg thrown carelessly over his assured Casca that this was no dream.

What had happened to him returned gradually to his fogged mind. How long he had been in the cave or what had happened during his long sleep, he didn't know. His mouth was dry, and his tongue felt the size of an ox's. He needed something to drink. Stiff muscles and joints cracking, he moved out from under the robes, careful not to wake the girl. As he moved out from under the robes, he could see, even in his dizzy state, that she was a real beauty. The flickering of the small fire cast gold and red shadows over her white skin, accenting the smooth valleys and curves of her body.

He moved to the opening of the cave and pulled his bear robe out of its hole to look outside. A blast of frigid air hit him, causing him to blink in renewed pain for a moment before he could replug the gap; then it passed. He looked for his gear and saw with some surprise that it was all still there. By the fire he found her pot. In it was water warmed by the flames. Casca drank it all in one motion, letting the fluid slide down to ease the parched membranes. Water had never tasted so good, not even during the time when he had been lost in the wastelands of the Persian desert.

Even that small effort wearied him. Silently, he returned to lie under the robes. Carefully, he placed her head on his arm and rolled over to face her, his mouth close to hers. He could smell her breath. It was like the fresh grass of spring, clean and sweet. His eyes closed, and he held the silver girl in his arms. They slept as two children do, holding each other for comfort against the dark.

With the dawn, the fire went out and they began to stir, their bodies seeking each other's warmth. As one, their eyes opened to look into the other's, the gray blue of the warrior's and the crystal lakes of the girl's. Casca forced words from his throat, dry and croaking from long disuse: "Welcome, whoever you are."

Ireina didn't answer immediately but moved closer to him and placed her lips on his. A still touching, devoid of passion, yet the touching she wanted, to show that she cared and needed him, the innocent kiss of a loving child who needed to be reassured.

They lay for some time until Ireina rose from their rough bed

to dress and rekindle a flame from the coals. Casca watched her
as she swept back a wayward tendril of hair. To him it looked a
liquid flow of purest silver.

She was happy for the first time in days, and the memory of
her abuse at the hands of Herac didn't matter anymore. It was
done with; she had more important things to think of now as she
prepared a meager meal of boiled dried meat and barley. She
was cooking for her man. It never occurred to her that he might
not want her to.

Casca flexed his muscles under the robe, trying to loosen
them. The ache was different this time. It was good to feel the
blood in his veins and the movement of muscle under his skin.
Without speaking, he rose to dress, leaving off his coat of steel
scales. Habit forced him, without being aware of it, to reach for
his sword. It was in good condition; rust hadn't eaten away too
much at the blade. He was glad of his habit of always oiling his
weapons, and here in the heights, it was not as damp, even
when it snowed. He placed the sword in its scabbard and lay it
back down.

Ireina watched him from the corner of her eye, wanting to ask
him a thousand questions yet knowing that it was better if she
waited.

Casca cleared his throat to find the words. "How long?"

She smiled at him. "How long what?"

"How long have been . . . ah, have I been asleep?"

She looked serious, trying to figure out how to give him an
answer. "I don't really know, but it has been a long time. My
great-grandmother knew of you when she was a child and told
of the way you saved our village and how you would come
again when danger threatened."

Casca thought for a time, but his mind was still not working
very quickly. "And has danger come again?"

She laughed, a tinkling sound. "You know that it has, else
why would you not still be asleep? That's a silly question. Now
eat." She shoved a wooden bowl at him. "You need to get your
strength back."

Casca obeyed her imperious demand and filled his mouth
with food. Not until he had finished did he notice that she ate
nothing. "Why don't you eat?"

Ireina flipped her hair back out of her face to lie in a tumbled
wave along her back. "I don't need much, and you do."

Casca took her sack and looked through it. There was only

enough for two or three small meals left. It meant they would have to leave the cave and go down into the valley if they were to have food.

Sitting cross-legged in front of her, across the fire, he said, "Tell me why you are here and what is going on below us."

Ireina's face took on a serious expression as she related the events in her village. She didn't say anything about what had happened to her; it was of no importance. She knew that the one who had hurt her would be punished without her saying anything. That was just the way it had to be now that he was awake.

Casca nodded his shaggy head in understanding. Nothing had changed, nor, he feared, would it ever. But there was something about this girl who trusted him that touched a distant memory of another he had known with hair like hers, and what they had shared. Without answering, he knew that he would do as she wished, but in order to do it, he needed some time to regain his strength, and only food could do that. Food and exercise, neither of which he could get in the cave.

From the way Ireina looked at him, he suspected that there might be exercise of some sort in the offing, but he didn't want to push it. Besides, he wasn't sure he had the strength for such an undertaking; she looked damned healthy. It would be best if that waited too.

CHAPTER FOUR

The close association with Ireina in the confines of the cave made it increasingly difficult for Casca to keep his eyes off her breasts and ripe hips. He knew that he was getting better.

Their food supply was gone. They had no choice but to go down into the valley. In a way he was relieved, for he knew that he wasn't ready to handle a girl such as this. It would be better if they waited before doing the inevitable.

Casca was still stiff. Muscles cracked and ached with every movement as he stuffed their few possessions into her sack. They would leave as soon as it was fully light. As they stepped out of the cave, he took one look back at what had been his refuge for so many years. He didn't know how many, and Ireina was of no help in the matter. There was a sense of dread as he took the first steps that would bring him into contact with the world below.

With Ireina trailing, he began the journey back down the path that led to the valley. Ice crunched under his feet as he broke through drifts piled against the wall of mountains by the storms that continuously raged in the upper regions, where ice was eternal and never shallow and not even an eagle flew through the vaulted corridors of wind and snow.

This was his first real excursion out of the cave, save for a few short trips to stretch out the cramped tendons that gave him a gait similar to that of an ape. The going was slow, but he knew that he was getting better. His legs were straightening out to normal, even if they were still somewhat weak. Ireina kept her face covered to the nose by a rag, leaving only her eyes exposed to the cold winds. By the time they reached the foot of the trail, Casca was covered in sweat under his moldy fur robes. It was too late to continue any farther; soon the dark would be on them.

They had to find shelter for the night. A small protected patch of ground between several large pines would give them cover.

He scraped away the surface crust of snow until he reached the soggy bed of pine needles below. Laying one of their robes over them, he cut branches to form a shelter, tying the ends together with strips of leather from her bag. It wasn't much, but it would do. In the morning he'd take a look at the village and then decide what they would have to do. He wished there had been some way he could have just taken her and headed south to the warm lands, but the passes were closed and the only food to be had was in the hands of the raiders. He would have to go there. He was still tired and knew that he wasn't up to anything near his full strength, but there were no other options. The raiders in the village would have to be disposed of. Stomach gurgling from hunger, Casca pulled her closer to him, put his arms around her, and slept uneasily, regretting that which would have to happen in the next days.

Several times that night he woke to the distant cry of a lone wolf singing in the distance. He knew that the cry was not that of a hunting animal but merely the death song of an old lone wolf. Waking with first light, he pulled himself out of the shelter, cringing when a pack of snow broke free from the branches overhead and slid down his back. He took out of their pack a few twigs of dried wood and used them to start a small fire in the mouth of the lean-to, where he sat slicing his old bearskin into strips and braiding the strands into a rope.

Ireina woke, eyes heavy with sleep, when the glow of the small fire warmed her face. There was no trace of concern in her features as she smiled pleasantly at her scowling companion. She knew that he would do all that was necessary.

Casca had to do something, and soon, and so he might as well get on with it. Grumbling for her to stay put until he returned, he took only his spear, sword, and hairy rope as he trudged out over the snow to where he could see several tendrils of smoke rising over the trees.

It took nearly three hours to cover the two miles to the clearing that in spring would be used by the villagers' cattle for grazing. From there he could see the puny log palisades that were supposed to provide the villagers with protection from the outside world. It had taken longer than he had thought it would to get this close. The day was too bright for him to attempt to cross the open space at this time; he would have to come back again after dark.

Returning the way he had come, he found Ireina sitting up, fresh as a spring flower; her hair was set in long silver braids around her head. The small brass pot she was stirring with a wooden spoon gave off a tempting aroma. Beside her, he saw the hide of a hare. While he had been scouting, she had been hunting, and with more success. They would eat this night.

He wanted to take a leg and start eating, but she made him wait till all the meat had boiled off the bones to thicken the broth. She knew that this would give him more strength than eating plain meat.

Once more their bodies supplied the warmth. He didn't sleep, afraid that if he did, he would wake too late to get into the village before light came. He wondered, too, about the strange girl whose head lay on his arm.

He wondered why she had such a fixation on him, such a blind belief that he could make all things turn out right. He looked away, up to the clear crisp winter sky, ablaze with pinpoints of light. What would she say if she knew all things about me? The question had no answer, but he was certain of one thing: Sooner or later pain or death came to all who got too close to him.

He rose while Orion was still high in the sky. He would have six hours before daylight. By then he would have to be finished with whatever he was going to do.

The return trip was the same as the one he had taken earlier. Getting up to the wall in the dark gave him no problems. The guards were not in evidence, though he was certain they were there. But if they were, as he figured, then they were interested in keeping an eye on the villagers inside the compound and not worried about anyone outside. They knew that it would be several months before the passes were clear enough of ice and snow for anyone to make it through.

He waited by the north corner of the wall to catch his breath. Straining his ears for any sound on the wall, he counted to a hundred. Hearing nothing, he used his bear rope to lasso one of the ends of the logs over him. Then he quickly climbed up to the top and dropped over with a thump. He slid on a patch of ice, nearly breaking a leg.

Casca froze where he was, sure that someone must have

heard the noise he had made. Nothing.

Once he had made certain that he hadn't been detected, Casca pulled his rope back up for future use. If there were guards on the walls, the best way to find them was to walk the perimeter till he found them. Moving slowly, bent over so that his body wouldn't show above the ramparts, half walking, half crawling, he slid forward on the slick walkway. At the junction of the north and east walls he caught sight of a dark figure hunched under his robe, sitting on a stool and trying to keep warm, facing the inside of the compound.

If that was the case, there was probably only one more guard on the walls at the junction of the south and west corners. Lowering himself down to his belly, Casca began to snake forward, one inch at time, never taking his eyes from his quarry. The guard never moved, except to wrap his robes around him a bit more snugly to keep out the chill.

Casca looked to the sky. He was in luck! The clouds were still covering the face of the winter moon. Slowly he rose to a half crouch, took a firm grip on his spear, and picked his spot: the junction where the neck joins the head. If he hit right, there should be no more noise from the guard than the escaping of air from his lungs. Drawing a deep breath, he set the point of the spear six inches from the guard's neck and then thrust forward, his full weight behind the spear. He drove the blade clear through the guard's neck and out the other side, pinning him to the wall. As he'd expected, there was little sound. The man died quickly and easily, making no fuss about it.

Now for the other man. He removed the dead man's helmet, a bell-shaped thing of hammered iron, exchanging it for his own. Then he took the already stiffening bloody robe from around the corpse and draped it over his own shoulders. He didn't have to use the same technique to reach the other sentry. This time he just walked up to the man casually, taking his time, keeping the robe where it covered all of his face but the eyes.

The remaining guard thought nothing of the approach of the familiar figure. It wasn't unusual for them to meet and talk a bit to pass the hours on watch. They knew that there was no real threat from the cattle sleeping in their huts. It would not have been a bad winter at all if Herac had been a bit more reasonable, and had not forced them to take turns standing watch in the cold. But the Greek had been right too many times for any of them to argue with him about it.

He gave a shiver and farted as he called out to what he thought was his friend. "How much longer till spring do you think it will be, Jorgaus? I have had it with this stinking pigsty and its ugly women and tasteless food. Perhaps Herac will take us south for the next season; then I won't have to endure another of these damned northern winters."

Casca was close enough to him to see the individual hairs in the man's beard. He grunted noncommittally to the guard's statements and then feigned a slip on the icy walkway, lurching forward and bumping into the sentry, who reached out a hand to steady him. Casca let his weight fall full on the man, dragging him down to the walkway with him.

The sentry started to laugh and then cursed at Jorgaus for being a clumsy ox, when a cold burning suddenly pierced through his abdomen. His screams were muffled by his robe being stuffed into his open mouth. The pain struck twice more, the last cut severing the aorta. He would have spat up a mouthful of blood if his mouth hadn't already been stuffed full with his robe.

Casca held him down, cursing the racket the dying man's heels made as they drummed on the walkway. Removing the knife, he pulled the body up to where he was sure it wouldn't roll off. Then he walked the perimeter of the compound one more time to make certain that there were no others on the wall whom he might have missed and to get a good look at the layout of the houses and storerooms. Using the ladder to get down to the bottom, he moved swiftly to the longhouse that was normally used for bachelor males. It was the largest structure in the village; it stood to reason that Herac and most of his men would be sleeping there.

It looked peaceful enough: snow on the thatched roofs, a covering a foot deep over the rest of the grounds, except for the most commonly used paths going from one hut to another. Smoke drifted up easily from chimneys to climb in gray columns to the sky. There was a smaller fenced enclosure near the north wall where the cattle and goats were kept, protected from the worst of the winds. One thing was missing. Dogs! Where were the village dogs? He would need to know that. If the animals started to bark, they could give him away. Not seeing any of them bothered him. He made one more pass around the walls, staying close to the sides. He didn't see or hear anything, neither dogs nor people.

Using what cover was available, he moved to the longhouse.

It was the same as any of the others in a hundred other villages. He risked a peek inside, having to bend over to get into the small entrance. Inside, he could see men lying about in robes and furs. Which one might be Herac he didn't know. Doing a fast count, he came up with the number. Twenty! He had taken care of two on the walls, which meant that he was missing a couple. They might be anywhere in the village, or they might be dead. He knew that one of the guards on the wall would have come down to wake the reliefs, and so there was little chance that he could catch another one on the outside.

First things first. He would need some help. He picked a hut at random and swung open the door. Inside, three figures were huddled together on the community bed, using each other for warmth. Two were women: the man's wife and her mother. At the intrusion, the man started to roll to his feet, thinking that one of the raiders had come by for another hit on his wife. But this time he was going to fight even if they killed him.

His attempt to rise was halted by a rough hand pushing him back to the bed. The beginnings of a wail from the women were silenced with a harsh, ''Shut your damned faces or I'll do it for you!'' Hissing at the man he held down, Casca whispered, ''I'm not with the bandits. Ireina has brought me to help you, but I need some help too. Are you with me?''

Molvai, grandson of old Hogar, nodded his head in agreement and then started to stutter when he recognized the features of his guest. It was the warrior from the cave. He was alive. So that was where Ireina had gone when she'd run off. He should have guessed. The girl had always had a soft spot in her head about the warrior, saying that he lived and would come down the mountain one day. His grandfather, too, had said the same thing.

Casca had to restrain the man to keep him from falling to his face in supplication. Jerking him back up, he said, ''Knock that shit off. I don't have time for it. You know which huts have men in them. Get them for me and be quiet about it. Also, I want to know if any of the raiders are sleeping in huts other than the longhouse.''

Molvai told his women to stay put. He and the warrior had things to do this night.

Once outside in the cold, Molvai started to move into the shadows, where he would be out of sight of the walls.

Casca spoke lowly. ''Don't worry, I've already taken them

out. There's no one on the walls but dead men.'' Shivering, he tried to get Molvai moving a bit faster. ''Now get me some men, and hurry. I don't know how much time we have. I'll wait near the longhouse. Bring them to me there, and be quiet about it.''

Molvai hastened to obey, racing from one hut to another. He would enter, wake the sleeping man, whisper in his ear, and then have to argue a few moments with him about the warrior. There were no weapons among the villagers except for one small knife that was permitted each family for the cutting of meat. All axes and other implements were kept by the raiders in the longhouse.

After the first three men, Molvai quit trying to explain about the warrior and just told the men that help had come and they were to gather outside.

Molvai led each man to Casca and then left to gather more, leaving each newcomer to wonder at the legend that had come true. The warrior had come down from his mountain to save them. Casca had difficulty restraining their outbursts of enthusiasm, till at last he felt it was necessary to thump a couple of them gently on the head to enforce silence.

Once the men of the village were gathered, he made up his mind about their course of action. In the words of the legion, it was always best to keep it simple.

They had to have some way to keep the men inside the longhouse from getting out. If they did, many of the villagers would die.

He whispered his orders to the men, sending them off to gather what he needed. The men went to their huts and storerooms. In less than twenty minutes they had returned, each bearing his load. Dry wood, precious oil, even articles of clothing were added to the growing pile. Logs were ripped from the palisade walls and brought to the entrances of the longhouse and placed in front of them, blocking any egress from the structure. Casca urged them to greater speed. The rest of the flammable items were placed evenly along the bottom of the longhouse, filling the area between the ground and the floor set on pilings. Oil was spread, and then basins of coals and fire were brought from a dozen houses. These were set under the wood at each corner to ensure a good even burn. Pitchforks and clubs were in the hands of all the males in case any of the raiders managed to get out of the longhouse. The fires began slowly at first and then grew

quickly as the small blazes caught and merged. Smoke began to
drift up and around the sides of the building, seeping into the interior. The sounds of coughing soon came from the inside.

Then a single cry of alarm woke the sleeping raiders. In a
panic, they rushed to the exits, only to find them blocked by the
logs. One man reached out his hand to try to push his way
through. Molvai grabbed the hand, pulling it out as far as he
could, and then began cutting it while a friend held it steady.
The short knife had a hard time sawing through the tendons between the wrist and hand, but patience prevailed and the hand
came off, accompanied by the screams of its former owner.
This served to keep the others inside from repeating the same
procedure.

The flames grew, spreading over the bottom of the
longhouse, filling the room with thick acrid smoke that ate at the
lungs. Herac tried to get his men organized. They took axes and
swords to hack at the walls, trying to cut a new way out. Several
fell, to lie on the floor where they had died, their lungs filled
with smoke.

Herac screamed in fear and rage for his men to break out.
They concentrated their efforts on one spot, and even the stout
logs began to give way to the frantic hacking of a dozen blades.
The first small gap in the walls soon grew into one that a man
could crawl through. One warrior attempted this, only to have
his skull smashed by a sweep from a pitchfork. This did not de-
ter the others. Fresh air entered, giving them a chance to
breathe. With increased strength, they attacked the hole, wid-
ening it even farther till it could take the whole body of a man. It
would have been best if they had expanded the opening even
more, but blinding panic was riding them. They had to get away
from the growing fires that were eating the floor out from under
them, threatening to collapse at any moment, sending them
down into the raging furnace beneath. The heat and flames
licked through cracks in the boards, searing their feet and climbing the walls of the longhouse, transforming the interior into a
flesh-blistering inferno.

Casca responded to Molvai's cry that the raiders were breaking out. Taking sword and spear, he rushed the spot in time to
see a man thrust his body out of the wall, ax in hand, clothes
smoldering. Wild-eyed, he'd struck down a villager who was
too slow in moving out of the way. Casca speared him as he
would have a pig.

Once the first man made his break, the others began to pour out, some on fire, others coughing and unable to breathe. Casca was concerned that too many of them would get out, but this wasn't to be. The floor of the longhouse collapsed, sending at least half of those inside crashing through to be roasted alive in the fire. The sounds of screams and sizzling flesh mingled with the new burst of oily smoke that came from human bodies being consumed.

Those who escaped the fire were mobbed by the village men, who had rallied their courage. Most of the warriors were still too weak from a lack of air and coughing to put up any resistance, even though they were better armed. They fell to flails, clubs, and pitchforks. Village men piled on them in twos and threes, hurling them to the ground to beat their brains out or stab them a hundred times with their short knives. It was bloody, unprofessional work, but it did the job. Herac was in the center of a group that burst out of the longhouse. He stood with two men, side to side, their backs to the flames and their eyes weeping rivers of smoke-agitated tears. Their skin showed the marks of fire: red welts over most of their exposed bodies. Their hair seemed near the point of bursting into flames.

Several men tried to get to them, forgetting to their eternal loss that they were facing killers who'd had a lot of practice at their craft. Herac and his surviving raiders cleared a space around them and then began to move out to the walls, where they hoped to be able to escape into the countryside. Three men, with weapons taken from dead raiders, attempted to face them down. They died in less time than the telling of it takes. Herac was no tyro at the fine art of slaughter and provided the base for his two surviving men to work from.

The villagers had formed a living wall around Herac and his men. The women had come out from the huts with the news that the raiders were being killed and had joined their men in trying to keep the raiders inside the walls. Several women threw themselves at the swordsmen and were cut down with no hesitation.

Casca had been inclined to let the men of the village do the rest of the dirty work for themselves. But once the women got into the act, it changed things for him. Women were just too temperamental, and he knew that they would only get killed and confuse things even more for their men. He had to take a hand in the mess once more.

Pushing his way through the mob, he smacked them with the

flat of his sword till they cleared a path for him directly in front of Herac.

The mob grew silent. The two men faced each other. Herac, hair smoking, skin black from ash and smoke, eyed this new danger through red-rimmed lids. Spitting out a hunk of phlegm, he grunted, ''You must be the cause of this. Why are you here? You obviously have nothing in common with these sheep who would be men.''

Molvai answered with a triumphant yell: ''This is the sleeper, the warrior from the mountains who has come to kill you.''

Casca wished he hadn't been so dramatic about the announcement. It was embarrassing.

Herac wasn't convinced. He'd heard the legend of the sleeping warrior but thought nothing of it. This man most probably was using the tale to his own advantage to take over power in the village.

Casca moved closer to the three, swinging his sword easily, point held low to the earth. He answered Herac's unspoken misgivings. 'What I am really doesn't matter because you're not going to leave here alive. So let's get it on and over with. I'm tired.''

Herac knew that he was a dead man. Even if the scar-faced warrior in front of him didn't kill him, it was unlikely that he would be able to get out alive with only two men. The rest of his band was being turned into charred stinking cinders in the burning coals of the longhouse.

Not waiting for any further dialogue, he struck, his two men alongside him. Casca was slower than he thought he'd be. The long years of idleness had stiffened muscles that refused to respond properly to the brain's signals to move. He knew what to do; he just wasn't fast enough. Herac opened up a slice in his gut, along the left side, cutting through the thin plates of the rusted scale armor. Casca closed with him, holding him to his chest. The two henchmen tried to cut Casca down from the sides but were dragged down by enraged villagers. The women were especially vengeful and received full payment for the use of their bodies and the deaths of their men and children.

Casca didn't complain about their assistance. He had all he could do to hold on to Herac. He was too weak to use his normal strength against the half Greek, but he did recall one of the things he had learned long ago about close-in fighting. Twisting his hip, he half turned to Herac's left. Letting go of his sword, he put his right arm under Herac's armpit and, with the twist, flipped him over his hip to land flat on his back, with the wind knocked out of him. Casca decided that it was time to end the show and gave Herac a full-bodied kick in the balls with his right foot. This kept his opponent immobile long enough for him to retrieve his sword and, without any further ado, cut the raider chief's throat to the applause and cheers of his village audience.

Casca was a bit disappointed in his performance, but the villagers thought he'd been sent from the gods to protect them and destroy their enemies. If he had said the word, they probably would have burned down their own village.

Casca yelled for them to quiet down and to put out the fires. He was tired from his labors and told Molvai to take a couple of men and go after Ireina. It was time she came home.

CHAPTER FIVE

Ireina returned with Molvai, not the least bit concerned or surprised. Why should she be? Hadn't everything turned out as she had always known it would? Her sleeping warrior had come down from the mountain and freed her people. There had never been any doubt of it in her mind. Why should she be surprised at what was only natural?

Casca was tired. Molvai turned over his own hut to him and Ireina, moving his family out to stay with one of his uncles. Casca didn't waste any time dropping off to sleep. The night had been long, and he was still weak. The fights had taken much from his slim reserves of strength, and he needed time to rebuild them. Ireina accepted the deference shown them both as no more than their due. She was the woman of the warrior, the one who had awakened him from his long sleep. She was his, and he was hers; of that there could be no doubt in anyone's mind.

While he slept, the villagers cleaned up the mess once the ashes had cooled enough for them to go in and haul out the charred bodies of the raiders. These they removed to the edge of the forest for the wolves and bears to feed on, provided that they had a taste for meat that was slightly overcooked.

There was a festive mood in the village for the next few days as they enjoyed the novelty of being their own masters again. Of Casca they saw little. He stayed to himself, resting and eating. He had no desire to be gawked at or pointed to. All he wanted was to be left alone for a time, until he readjusted to being among the living.

Ireina helped in that respect. He was glad that he had waited a few days, gathering strength before he gave in to the inevitable. For him it was a pleasant if exhausting joining. For Ireina it was the final establishing of her claim to him, and she was deter-

51

mined that her man would have no reason to look elsewhere for companionship.

Once he did come out into the open. The villagers wanted to make him their chief. This he refused gently but firmly. He wanted no responsibility for them. Ireina gave him a disapproving look but said nothing. If he didn't want to be chief, he must have a good reason.

His reason was that he knew that he couldn't stay with them. Once the passes were open, he would have to leave. It was a constant irritation to be watched, pointed to, and whispered about. He had to give orders that offerings were not to be left at his door anymore, but that didn't stop the custom completely. It was not unusual for him to find a piece of smoked meat or a few eggs when he opened the door. If it had just been food, he wouldn't have been so concerned, but there were also signs that the offerings had been made to him in what they thought of as his aspect of being a half god. Small clay figurines of the earth mother or other local deities were usually placed near the offerings.

Casca did not wish to be anyone's god. It was too great a burden. The only good thing about the way everyone treated him was that he was able to sit on his ass for the rest of the winter, taking it easy. Just as the weather was beginning to warm, he had a moment of consternation when he noticed that Ireina was beginning to put on a little weight and walked around most of the time with a smug expression on her face. It didn't take him long to figure out that she was pregnant. This bothered him a bit. He knew that he wasn't able to sire any offspring and wondered whether she'd been messing around.

A little conversation with Molvai explained the circumstances of the rape by Herac. But, he figured, what the hell? If she wanted to think it was his, why not?

It was spring when the child was born to Ireina: a fine healthy boy with fair features and dark eyes. Casca had by this time come to think of the new arrival as his own and was as anxious as any expectant father.

For him it was a new experience to put out a rough finger and feel the small fingers of a baby tug at them and try to suck them.

He swore that he would give the baby all that a father could. He would have stayed in their high mountain valley if the villagers had accepted him as a normal man and not some type of supernatural being. The women would bring their children to him and plead for him to touch their heads to bring them luck. The way they treated his son was no different. The baby was an object of awe and wonder. If they stayed there, the child would have no chance to grow up normally. When the day came that he discovered that he was only mortal and not the child of a demigod, it would bring him nothing but grief.

When Demos was six months old, Casca decided that he was strong enough for them to leave the mountains. He hated to do it but felt that there was no other choice. Ireina didn't care. As long as she was with him and had her child, she would go anywhere without complaint. Her dreams were all coming true.

The horses and what silver the raiders had had on their bodies, Casca claimed as his due for services rendered. There were no complaints from anyone. The only problem was that they didn't want to let him go. But they also knew there was no way to stop him. He did make one concession, promising to return one day.

With Ireina on a horse behind him and Demos nestled in his scarred arms, they began to descend to the warm lands below, where snow seldom fell and winds were gentle.

The horses he sold at Aquileia. The money he got for them was enough for them to live comfortably for several months. He wanted this time to watch Demos grow. Every day was a new adventure for him. The first unsure steps rapidly passed into overconfident little stumbling steps. Casca was constantly afraid that Demos was going to break his head open every time the baby climbed to its feet. Ireina took all this in stride. Like most mothers, she knew instinctively that her child's rubbery, flexible body was nearly indestructible and that in spite of all the falls and bruises, he would grow stronger each day.

The only fly in the ointment was that with each day their reserve of money grew lower. What work Casca was able to find was a poor supplement to the growing needs of his family. For a time he worked as a bouncer in several local taverns, until his reputation grew so bad that it started driving off customers and he was fired. The only other work to be had which paid as well would have taken him away from Ireina and Demos. That he tried to avoid for as long as possible, for he had found great pleasure in the growing child. He took an inordinate amount of pride in each of the babe's accomplishments, such as climbing to his feet by himself. Casca swore that anyone could see that never had a child done such things so young or so well.

Ireina never lost her childlike simplicity or her belief that Casca and she were part of some fairy tale. No matter how many times he tried to reason with her, she would just smile smugly as if to say, ''Go on and say anything you want to. I know the truth, and nothing will change it.'' Sometimes he wondered if perhaps she'd been hurt more than was obvious by her rape. She never mentioned the raiders or Herac again, and if he brought up the subject, she just looked at him with a blank expression and went on with whatever she was doing.

He had no problems with Ireina. It wasn't that she was stupid. There were just some things that she didn't understand, and he was foremost among them. In their daily life she was pleasant and attentive and could argue with the butcher over the price of a piece of meat with the best of them. He managed to keep them with shelter and food on the table until Demos was five by taking any work he could find. His strong back was always welcome where fields had to be cleared of stones or wood cut and hauled to different cities, but that was only enough for them to barely survive on, and he wanted more for them than just an existence of living hand to mouth.

Casca knew that soon he would have to find better-paying employment. He dreaded the idea, but there was no way to avoid it. Inflation and rising prices had rapidly depleted their resources. He was going to have to go back to work, and there was only one way he would have a chance to make enough to give him what he wanted for Ireina and Demos.

He would have to sell his sword for a time. Then, when they had saved enough, he'd buy a farm for them, where they could be kept away from the evil of the world. He also knew that the day would come when he would have to walk away from them, to leave them on their own. When that happened, he intended for them to be taken care of. That was a hateful thought but one that couldn't be ignored. Perhaps this time he would be able to do it gently and not have them hurt because of him.

He would have to make a lot of money to accomplish that. He had wished several times that he had been a good businessman, but he had no talent for it and knew it.

There were not many places where he could get a good price for his labor. He would have to go where they were hiring. It wouldn't have done any good to go to Rome, which was ruled by barbarians and had little need of paid mercenaries. The only place he knew that had the money to afford professional mercenaries was Constantinople. There were always more trouble spots than the regular legions of the Eastern Empire could take care of. He would have to sign on with one of the mercenary captains.

He didn't like the idea of taking Ireina and Demos with him to Constantinople, but he didn't want to leave them where he couldn't take care of them in the event of trouble. The world was as dangerous a place as it had been under Gaius Caesar.

Others were at work also. In accordance with the orders of the Elder, men had been sent out from every province and city to question, to follow every rumor about any man of unusual abilities or extreme longevity. The description of Casca was indelibly impressed on their memories. Every scar-faced man was subject to question.

It was while tracing down the origin of one of these stories that followers of the Lamb came to the village where Casca and Ireina had lived. When the passes opened up to the highlands, merchants and travelers came and went as usual. The villagers delighted in the telling of the story of their own special demigod who watched over them. Most who heard the story took it as no more than that, just another of the wild fables that people who are isolated for much of the year through long winters seem to produce in endless quantities. The men of the Brotherhood did not take the story as a fable. When Molvai sat with them, he told them of the strength of the sleeper and of his scars, especially the one that ran from the edge of his left eye to the corner of his mouth, and how another circled his left wrist like a bracelet.

Molvai enjoyed the effect his story had on the men who sat in his hut, the astonishment on their faces when he told of the manner in which the gray-blue eyes of the sleeper could strike terror into the heart of an enemy. The listeners showed no signs of disbelief when he related the story of Casca and how he first came to the valley and finally went to the ice mountains to sleep and wait until he was needed once more—how he was finally brought back to life in their hour of need by the girl Ireina, who became his wife and bore him a son. Molvai knew that it was possible that the child was not that of the sleeper, but it sounded better in the telling if he ignored that possibility.

When his visitors left, he knew that he had told the tale well. They fairly rushed with excitement to their animals to go back down through the passes.

The word was sent to Gregory that after three years they had succeeded. They had not found the beast, true, but they were closer, and it was now known for certain that he was real. Gregory called the men who had visited Molvai to him. He had to hear the story firsthand from their own mouths. If they lied or exaggerated, he would have their hearts torn from their living bodies.

They were taken to see him in the same catacombs used for their religious services. They did not know his name or face, only that they were being permitted to be in the presence of the master.

Gregory was troubled by the tale, especially the part about the child. That was a problem they had not faced before; it cast a new light on several issues that would have to be resolved. But first he had to know where the beast was hiding. Now that he was slowed down by a woman and child, it shouldn't be too difficult to locate him. The animal had only one way of earning a living, and that would narrow the scope of their search greatly. They would be able to concentrate on those who had need of killers to hire. There Casca would go sooner or later, and when he did, he would be found.

The messengers were sent back to their diocese with the blessings of the Elder, and the word was spread of their plan to locate the beast. Patience, patience, patience. In time the beast would be found and with him something perhaps even more dangerous, the child of the beast.

CHAPTER SIX

Sicarus

Casca stood before the great walls of Constantinople, his arm around the shoulders of Ireina. She was carrying their son; his head was resting against her shoulder. He mumbled sleepily that he wanted to go to bed. Casca reached over and ran a hand through his dark curly hair. "Soon, my son, soon you'll have a warm bed."

Going in front of Ireina, he forced a path for them through the throngs entering the huge gates of bronze and hardwoods. Pushing past an Arab merchant in flowing robes and turban, he found himself in front of a young bright-faced officer of the city guard.

Raising his face, the young officer found his eyes locked on those of the scar-faced man. Casca leaned over the table where the young man was taking a count of those who entered or left through his gates each day. "Where can I find quarters for my family?" he asked.

The boyish centurion tried to remember his official position, though his voice cracked a bit as he responded to this brusk, somewhat intimidating questioner. "Before I answer that, what is your name and your business here?"

He didn't have to ask the man's occupation. The deep scars on the arms, hands, and wrists made it quite clear that the man was a fighter. But he had to observe regulations. Orders stated that anyone entering the city was to be questioned, and those who looked to be of special interest were to be reported to the praefectus vigilum, who would in turn review the list, weeding out those of no real interest, and then submit a list of the remaining names to the eparch, who was directly under the thumb of the magister officorum, otherwise known as Gregory the Eunuch.

The centurion didn't know the reason, but for the last few years they had been required to make daily reports on the comings and goings of strangers, especially those who appeared to be warriors of a particular type: thick-bodied, heavily muscled men with scars and light eyes. It was a pain in the ass to do it every day.

Casca responded wearily and a bit snappishly to the questions. "I have come to seek employment with Sicarus the mercenary, and I am called Casca. Anything else you wish to know, young master?" Although the words were respectful enough for one addressing a member of the Illustrii, the tones left something to be desired. However, the slightly built officer decided that the man was obviously ill bred and didn't know any better. Therefore, he would be gracious and not press the issue.

Affecting a slight tone of superior contempt, he told Casca, "You will want the street of the potters. That is where most of the hirelings of Sicarus stay. They can direct you further."

Casca nodded and left, with Ireina trailing in his wake as he separated the mob in front of them. The centurion made a mental note to set an appointment to have his hair curled and perfumed; the other note was to tell his corporal to transfer the name of Casca to the list that was to be sent to the praefectus. He remembered the hair but forgot the other matter till he was already being relieved of duty. For him to send the note in late would have reflected on his capabilities. Besides, the man, whatever his name, was just another brute of no importance. Best to leave things alone.

Casca and his family walked through the streets of the city of Constantine, treading over stones that had known the passing of countless legions and conquerers. It was the largest city in the world west of the thousand-mile wall of China. The streets were busy with hawkers crying their wares to wives, slaves, and tourists. Caravans of camels and mules left their droppings on the cobblestones to collect on the feet of unwary pedestrians.

Casca took Demos from Ireina, who was showing signs of fatigue, though she made no complaint. Holding his son cradled in his left arm, he led the way to the street of potters without having to ask directions. He had been in Constantinople when it was known as Byzantium and a half dozen times since then. Unless they'd rearranged the streets, there would be no problem finding his way through the maze. Most of those on the streets gave way readily to the man with the child. They recognized a warrior when they saw one, and as most were simple folk, they had no desire to hinder one who lived by the sword, which was well enough, since Casca was tired and a bit ill tempered from their journey.

It took nearly an hour of wending in and out of narrow byways and bazaars to reach the street of potters, which lay next to the main market where food, weapons, silks, and slaves were offered for sale in an endless stream. When Casca came to a stuccoed, three-storied building with the sign of a broken lance over it, he turned inside.

The inn was not of the caliber frequented by the Illustrii of the capital, but it was familiar enough to him. All inns were basically the same, differing only in the degree of cleanliness and the quality of the food and clientele. He handed Demos back to Ireina before entering the darker confines of the hostel. It took a few moments for his eyes to adjust to the change in light from the glare outside to the darker smoky insides of the Broken Lance. He saw several men sitting at tables, eating and drinking, who wore the mark of fighters on them: scars on faces and bodies, which they wore as soldiers did their medals of valor. There was harshness to their voices and manner that was universal to those of their ilk.

They also watched him. Eyes sized him up quickly; then they looked at his woman, admiring the silver hair and firm breasts; then they returned to the man again before deciding to leave her and him alone for the time being.

Casca didn't like bringing Ireina and Demos to such a place, but he had to find employment. Their money was nearly gone, and Demos ate more than he did. Ireina kept close to his back, not liking the looks given her by the patrons. Grabbing a serving wench by her arm, Casca asked where the master of the inn could be found. Ireina liked even less the look the serving girl gave her man than she did those given her. She made up her mind to keep a close eye on Casca while they were here.

Following the girl's pointing finger, Casca moved across the plank floors to the one fire, where an obese man with a greasy apron was basting a goat on a spit. Polonius cursed and stuck a finger in his mouth to ease the pain where a touch of flame had licked him when the stranger behind him had startled him.

Still sucking his finger, he tried to speak, but the words only came out in a childish gibberish. Casca stopped the man's mumblings by pressing his fingers deep in his collarbone until he had his full attention.

"Rooms, landlord! I want a clean room for my woman and child."

Polonius eyed his potential guest, taking in the travel-stained clothes and the pack on the broad back, which he knew without asking contained the man's armor. Looking over Casca's shoulder, he saw Ireina and Demos. It was unusual. Very few mercenaries ever brought their women and children with them. But as long as he could pay, it made no difference.

Casca knew what the innkeeper was thinking, and after they had haggled long enough to satisfy honor, a price was agreed upon and Casca was finally able to take Ireina and Demos up to the second floor, where she was able for the first time in weeks to lay her body on a semiclean bed and place Demos down where the child could stretch out his legs and then curl them up again and sink into a deep sleep.

Casca moved a thin cover over Demos and Ireina, telling her to stay where she was until he returned, emphasizing that she was not to open the door for anyone. Ireina nodded her head in agreement. She was too tired to think about going anyplace, not even downstairs. All she wanted was the incredible luxury of curling up next to her son and holding him while they slept the day around.

When Casca left the inn, returning to the crowded streets, he did a mental tally of the few coins left in his purse. If he didn't get some money soon, he might have to knock a tourist in the head. From the innkeeper he'd gotten directions to where Sicarus stayed. He had an office in an unused portion of the old imperial barracks, near the western wall. It took nearly another hour to cross to that side of the city.

He could tell at once that Sicarus ran a pretty tight ship. Usually mercenaries were a pretty sloppy lot, but he was challenged very professionally by a member of some obscure tribe of barbarians who asked all the right questions and showed more good manners than the centurion had shown at the city gate. Once he had his questions answered as to why Casca was there, he politely told his guest to take a seat on a bench reserved for such things just outside the guard post, saying, "Someone will come for you in a moment."

The guard quickly sent a half-naked beggar boy off to find whoever it was that would come for him. Casca was glad to sit down for a few minutes; his feet were sore, and he was tired.

He had nearly dozed off by the time two armed men showed up. They looked the same as the one who had told him to take a seat: sharp, clean-looking men with the aura of discipline about them, even if their arms and clothing were not of a uniform type. One of them, obviously a Greek, nodded for him to join them. They placed themselves one on either side of him, leading Casca across a compound where once soldiers of the emperors had trained but which was now rented by the mercenaries of Sicarus for close-order drill and weapons practice. A number of men were squared off practicing casts with javelins, while others sparred with blunted swords. It reminded him of his own days when he had trained under the watchful eye of Corvu the Lanista, of the school of the Galli, when he had been a gladiator.

The mercenaries led him to a stone two-storied building where two others stood guard with spears. Once there, they took his sword and knife before permitting him to enter the building. Obviously, Sicarus was a man with enemies. They gave his weapons to a black slave who placed them in a box near the doorway.

Casca's escort stayed with him as they walked down a long hall past several doors before stopping at one near the far end and knocking. A smooth clear voice commanded them to enter.

Sicarus sat behind a plain desk, going over his accounts; the cost of maintaining his three hundred men was high. He was well formed, handsome in a dark serious manner, of average height. Hair graying at the temples was held back with a plain silver band. The face was intelligent, that of a man who made few mistakes. Casca had no doubts about the abilities of Sicarus to lead. He carried authority like part of his skin.

One of the guards removed himself to the outside of the door, and the other stayed a bit to the rear of Casca. Both waited for Sicarus to finish his inspection of the new candidate.

Aiming his quill at Casca like a lance, he asked his questions quickly and expected responses to be delivered the same way. Casca gave them back in the order they were asked. Although he evaded any question pertaining to time, he had no difficulty providing Sicarus with more than enough information to let the man know he'd had plenty of experience. The fact that there were areas he chose not to elaborate on took nothing away from him. Most of those who came to sell their swords had reasons for not wishing their entire life story to be known.

Sicarus knew how to read his men. He could tell those who killed for pay and those who killed for pleasure. There were some like this one who did not really fit into either category. They killed because they had to, receiving no pleasure from the taking of life but not avoiding it, either.

Sicarus knew that he wanted this man from first sight. His eyes didn't have either the lackluster of the brute or the burning passion of those who walked the borderline of madness. This man would be as steady as his grayish eyes. But it was always best to test your instincts from time to time.

"Have you ever fought against vandals before?"

The question was plain but loaded. Casca nodded and responded without emotion, "Enough to respect the throwing ax."

Sicarus pointed to a shield hanging on the wall of the office. "To whom did that belong?"

Casca glanced at it out of the corner of his eye. The sun symbol in the center boss was not that of Rome. "Persian. It's the shield of an officer of the Persian light cavalry, but it's an old one. That style hasn't been used for many years, but you can still find them among some tribesmen on the frontier."

Those answers said much for the man. If a warrior knew both the Vandals and Persians and had survived, he was definitely worthwhile, and Sicarus wanted only the best. That was why he could demand and get the price he did for his services. "I would guess from your build that you're either a sword or spear man. Which do you prefer?"

Casca shrugged his sloping shoulders. "I have had experience with both but favor the sword."

Sicarus dismissed the remaining guard with the message to find Hrolvath and bring him to the training ground. The man saluted with hand to chest and left to obey Sicarus's order.

Rising from behind his desk, Sicarus walked closer to Casca. Their eyes were on the same level. "There is one other thing to do before I will accept you into my company. Everyone that joins me must go through it. Come with me."

Casca followed Sicarus as the leader of the mercenaries led him out to the training compound. He had a feeling that he knew what the test was going to be, and he didn't blame the mercenary leader for it. It was a good way to weed out the phonies in a hurry rather than find that they couldn't do the job when your life depended on it.

Sicarus cried out for the attention of the other men training on the grounds. "Comrades, I have with me one who would join our illustrious company of gentlemen. Shall we see if he is worthy of us?"

The men on the grounds stopped what they were doing to laugh at their leader's description of them as gentlemen, responding to his question with catcalls and jeers of, "Let me try him on for size."

Sicarus took Casca to a weapon rack and told him to pick out anything he liked. Casca removed several swords of varying length from the rack, swinging them to and fro in his hand till he found one of the proper weight and length. The weapons were not for true fighting, as the edges and points were dulled, but they could still do enough damage to cripple a man.

Several calls of, "Don't hurt yourself, darling; those things are not toys," accompanied Casca's selection. He smiled gently at their jokes. He looked overhead at the afternoon sun. It could get sweaty today, he thought. He removed his tunic, slipping it over his head. At the sight of the twisted muscles and myriad scars that decorated his body, the jeering ceased, turning to hushed whispers of awe. Whatever the man was, he had without doubt seen more than his fair share of action.

Some calls picked up again as the cry of "It's Hrolvath that's going to test him" went through the men.

Casca had figured out by now that he was going to have one of the local boys' favorite badasses, but he hadn't expected anything like the man now pushing his way through the fighters. Hrolvath was about the same height as Casca but had golden hair hanging in waves over his tanned shoulders. When Sicarus had told his man to bring him Hrolvath, Casca had thought that because of the name, he would be facing one of those monstrous Germans or Goths, not this delicate man-boy with his beardless face and delicate long fingers.

He hadn't survived all these years by not knowing when something sneaky was going on. If Sicarus wanted him to go against this child warrior, there had to be something about the boy that made him special. He was not going to get careless. He was nearly twice as broad in the shoulders as his tender opponent and could have snapped his girlish neck with a twist of one scarred hand.

The boy was beautiful. If he'd been a slave girl, he would have brought thousands in gold at any bazaar in the world. Sicarus had a smug expression as he watched the consternation and confusion run over Casca's face.

It was clear that the men around them were familiar with the routine, for they formed a large circle without being told to and quieted down. Sicarus motioned for Hrolvath to come to him. The boy broke free of his admirers to join Sicarus and his guest.

Casca watched the boy with interest as he came toward them. You could sometimes tell a lot about a man by the way he moved. Hrolvath strode to them with the smooth confidence of a healthy young panther. Although he looked like one who preferred men to women, there was nothing effeminate about his movements. Every swing of his legs and arms was a study in effortless grace. As he neared, Casca saw that the boy's cheeks were not completely smooth. There was a scar running down the side of his face from the temple to below the ear on the left side. The scar only served to accent the beauty of the young man. His eyes were bright blue and clear, sparkling with good humor and love of life. He greeted Sicarus with a tone that said the boy was truly fond of the master of the mercenaries.

"*Ave,* and good morrow to thee, master. Who is this you have with you?"

Everything about the boy was so perfect that Casca was beginning to get a bit irritated. Even his voice was that of master singer, clear and chiming. No one had a right to be that perfect.

Sicarus introduced Casca. "This is one who wishes to join us. I believe he has merit and would have you put him to the test."

Hrolvath smiled pleasantly at Casca. "I would be pleased to do so."

He extended his hand in a friendly manner to be shook by Casca, who was surprised at the strength in the small hand and wrist. The boy was no weakling; there was strength in those thin limbs.

Hrolvath looked over the body of his challenger admiringly but was not the least bit intimidated by it. He observed with the same good-natured tones to Sicarus, "I believe you're right. If those wounds are any indicator, the man is clearly a survivor of many combats. I like him!''

Casca had a feeling the boy wasn't lying. Hrolvath seemed completely sincere in his words. Casca wasn't sure the boy knew how to lie. On his part, he merely tried to grunt as good-naturedly as he could.

Moving to the weapon rack, Hrolvath removed a sword that Casca had wondered briefly about when making his own selection. It was a thin blade, about the width of man's thumb and nearly a foot longer than his own weapon. Like his own stubbier sword, the point was dulled, as was the edge.

Hrolvath swung the sword in a graceful sweep, twisting it in a smooth circle. Then he stopped to test the flexibility by bending the point in till the sword formed an arc. Casca didn't like the looks of it. He had never seen a sword quite like this one, and from the boy's actions, he knew it was not a toy.

Hrolvath gave the sword to Sicarus to hold for him as he tied his shoulder-length hair back with a strip of soft red leather to keep it out of his eyes. Sicarus was grinning from ear to ear through the whole process, obviously having a good laugh at a show he'd seen and enjoyed many times before.

Casca was becoming a bit impatient. He didn't like being played with. Sicarus gave Hrolvath back his sword and stepped away from the two men, with orders not to begin until he gave the word. They were to stop instantly on his command. He warned Casca that if he didn't obey instantly, he would regret it. This was not a kill contest.

The circle formed by the watchers was about fifty feet in diameter. Casca and Hrolvath went to the center, keeping a space of about five feet between them. At the word to begin from Sicarus, they began to circle each other, taking their time. Casca held his blade well to the front, moving sideways. He was still uneasy about the long flexible sword of Hrolvath and how it was to be used.

Hrolvath, on his part, moved with easy grace, lightly swinging his long toothpick back and forth in the air, using only his wrist. Casca moved in cautiously, probing the strengths and weaknesses of Hrolvath's guard. Hrolvath didn't seem to be very interested in the process. Almost with disdain he used his weaving weapon to fend off Casca's probes with light flicks, using only enough force to deflect the attack, not block it.

It came as a shock to Casca that even as he increased the tempo of his attack, Hrolvath never changed his attitude or seemed to use any more effort to ward him off. It was beginning to get a bit aggravating. The audience began to renew its jibes at his feeble efforts. Hrolvath smiled sympathetically, as if he hated to have to embarrass his clumsy, sweaty opponent.

Perhaps because of his sympathy, Hrolvath decided to begin his counterattack. Then Casca found out the secret behind that long, thin toothpick. It never left his face. The extra length and the lightness of the blade made his heavy counters nearly useless. He would block it with a strong counter only to have the flexible length whip back to the front of his face, where it constantly threatened his throat and eyes.

If he'd had a shield or even a small buckler, he might have been able to use that as cover to get close enough inside the darting point to where his shorter sword could have been of some use.

Frustration, anger, and embarrassment ate at him. His inability to make even one effective attack was humiliating. It was all he could do to keep the thin sword from pricking him with every graceful sweep or lunge that Hrolvath felt like making. He was facing something new in the art of swordplay and had no defense against it by using the methods he had been taught. If the things he normally used didn't work, he would have to try something they didn't expect.

Hrolvath extended his arm fully, causing the blunted point to make small circles in front of Casca's eyes. Casca shifted his grip so that he was holding the handle of his sword reversed. As he dodged down to avoid the darting shaft, Sicarus saw this and only had time to wonder momentarily before he saw the reason for the strange grip. As Casca completed his half turn to get away from Hrolvath's sword point, he drew his sword arm back and then thrust forward, casting the blunt end of the haft like a javelin. The butt of the sword struck solidly into Hrolvath's stomach, knocking the wind from him and causing him to lower his guard for a moment. When he did, Casca was on him, one hand holding Hrolvath's sword wrist, the other on the boy's neck, twisting so that Hrolvath lost both his balance and his sword. Casca had the boy where he couldn't move, and if he had chosen to, he could have easily killed the young man simply by breaking his neck. But he knew that this wasn't a kill contest, and he was more angry at himself than at the young mercenary.

Sicarus, just to be certain, hurriedly called an end to the contest. There was muttering from among the onlookers at the trick Casca had used against their favorite. He gave the boy his hand, pulling him back to his feet.

Laughing and holding his tender throat, Hrolvath hugged the big Roman. To Casca's embarrassment, he cried out happily, "You certainly taught me something with that. I won't be quite so confident next time."

Casca grinned a bit sheepishly, saying, as all who watched knew anyway, "You didn't leave me many choices, and I know that you could have impaled me on that pig sticker you call a sword whenever you chose to. Your only mistake was in waiting too long and playing with me. That gave me time to think. But you could have won the match any time you chose to, and we all know it."

Sicarus was pleased at the exchange taking place between the two men. It was good to have men admit their mistakes and weaknesses; then they could do something about them. He'd thought that Casca would not have a chance against the thin, lightning-fast swordplay of young Hrolvath. No one had ever beaten Hrolvath, not even he. But the Roman had shown that he could think on his feet, even when angry.

CHAPTER SEVEN

Mercenary

Once the other mercenaries saw that their chieftain had accepted Casca, as had Hrolvath, their attitude changed radically. They began to say that perhaps he was a good fellow, though there was a touch of envy behind some of their words. None of them had ever thought of taking the same course of action as he had against Hrolvath, or they would have done it too.

Hrolvath bade Casca farewell, leaving him with the promise to meet again. Sicarus took over from there, taking Casca back with him to his office, where he explained the rules of his brigade. He had great pride in his men and their performance. They were, in his opinion, the best independent force in the world, and he expected all his men to act as such. There would be no looting unless express permission had been given, and rape was forbidden on the pain of death. However, in their contract, they did have first selection of all captured women, and these, of course, could not be considered rape victims since they would become the property of their new masters.

The pay was good: twenty silver denarii per month and a one-third share of all captured loot. There were also additional benefits for a man if he lost an arm, hand, or leg or his life. Sicarus would not have any of his men thrown out to starve because of wounds received in his service.

Sicarus released Casca to return to the inn, telling him to inform the master of the inn that his room bills were to be put on the mercenary's account and billed to him until Casca received his first pay. Then it would be deducted a bit at time till it was made up. Casca left, feeling all in all that he had made a good choice in joining this company of mercenaries and their dapper leader. The man was fair and seemed to have high ethics for one involved with such a bloody business. He had said nothing of the forthcoming campaigns against the Vandals in Africa, but Casca figured that he probably thought there was no need to go into detail at this time. Everyone knew that the campaign couldn't begin until after the rains ended and Belisarius came back from Italy.

It was nearing sundown when he reached the Inn of the Broken Lance and pushed his way inside. Upstairs, he knocked on the door to wake Ireina, but it was Demos who came and unlatched it, letting him in. Casca gathered the boy in his arms, gave each of his sleepy eyes a kiss, and put him back in bed beside his mother, pulling the cover over them. He undressed and slid in beside them. It could wait until the morrow before he told Ireina of the day's events. They would just sleep this night, the three of them together. Demos rolled over the top of his mother, sticking his rear in Casca's stomach, snuggling down between his father and his mother to sleep, content that all was well in his world.

The sounds from the inn below increased with the dark as wine and beer flowed more freely, but the noise was lost on the sleepers upstairs. They never heard the fight that killed a Syrian sailor from Rhodes, nor heard the door being broken down in a fight between some of the mercenaries and a squad of the imperial guards who tried to establish their authority by attempting to arrest two of them. The guards returned to their barracks minus two swords, a couple of breastplates, and all their money. Most of them felt they had gotten off easy and made no complaint of their treatment to their superiors. It would not look good on their records to be beaten in such a humiliating fashion by the hirelings of Sicarus.

Casca was awakened by a repeated, insistent rapping on his door that forced open his unwilling eyes. He removed Demos's foot from his throat and stumbled over to the door, where he opened it, ready to heap abuse and verbal filth on whoever it was who had the temerity to wake a man at such an ungodly hour.

It was almost as bad, facing what he thought would be the foul, greasy landlord, as it was to stand there and be bathed in the glory of white perfect teeth in a smiling face wishing you a good morning and sticking rolls of fresh-baked bread, still warm from the oven, under his nose; along with half a wheel of the overripe goat cheese of the Bedouins, considered a delicacy in the capital.

Hrolvath, when he saw that he had disturbed Casca's slumber, began to apologize profusely. Then, over Casca's shoulder, he saw the figures of Ireina and Demos still in bed. His face blushed with embarrassment as he withdrew, saying that Sicarus wished for Casca to present himself to him in his office within the hour.

It took a few minutes for Casca to get dressed, clear the crap from his brain, and tell Ireina to wake up. He left the rest of his remaining supply of small coins for her to buy some food for the child while he was gone.

It was near the hour of midday when he and Hrolvath reached the mercenary camp. He noticed, in contrast to the previous day, that there were no men on the exercise field. From the area of the stables he could hear the whinnying of horses and the clatter of equipment. Several groups of men passed in a rush, their faces red and sweaty with excitement. He didn't have to be told what was happening. He had experienced the same thing too many times not to know the signs that there was war in the wind; these men were preparing for battle.

This was confirmed when he saw Sicarus approaching them, accompanied by a secretary to whom he was dictating at a rapid pace his needs of the next weeks: grain, spare horses, leather to repair harnesses and equipment. Spying Casca, he stopped his dictation momentarily and waved for Casca to join him as he made the rounds of the camp.

"I am sorry that I had to call on you this way, but things have changed radically overnight. Belisarius has returned, and we are to leave as soon as possible, by ship, as the vanguard to secure a bridgehead by which he may land his main force, which will be a couple of days behind us. He has made an agreement with the barbarians in Rome not to interfere with our operations in Africa if the emperor will recognize them as the legal and lawful rulers of those parts of the old empire they currently hold."

He gave another spurt of instructions to his secretary and then continued his dialogue with Casca. "I know that you have your woman and child with you. No! Don't interrupt me. I have a small farm not far from here where my own wife resides. I

would deem it an honor if your lady and son would stay with her
while we are gone. I am sure that your mind would rest much
easier to know that they would not be left alone in this city. And
I know that my lady would be pleased for the company and especially the presence of the child, as we do not yet have one of
our own, to our sorrow. If this is agreeable to you, I will have
slaves escort them under guard to my farm tomorrow morning
before we sail.''

Casca nodded his head in agreement, though he found it a little difficult to digest everything as fast as Sicarus threw it at
him. But he did know that the master of mercenaries was an
honorable man, and he would certainly be more comfortable in
his mind if he didn't have to think of Ireina and Demos being
left alone in a city of this size and nature, where almost anything
could happen to the unwary or innocent.

Sicarus beat him to his unasked questions. ''We leave on the
morning tide to rendezvous up the coast, where we will be met
by Belisarius himself, who will give us our battle orders; from
there, on to Carthage. Now go and spend the day with your
woman and child and present yourself to me on the docks by the
grain houses one hour after dawn. Oh, by the way—'' he removed a small sack of clinking coins from his waistband and
tossed them to Casca. ''—give these to your lady. It should be
enough to cover her expenses until we return or until you are
able to send her more from your wages if the campaign takes
longer than I think it will.''

Ireina was up and moving, Demos by her side. The two were
sharing a breakfast of cheese and olives, washed down with
fresh goat's milk. Demos ran to Casca when he saw him enter
the room and wrapped his chunky little arms around one of
Casca's large thighs to catch a ride as his father walked.

Casca removed the rider from his leg with one hand, grabbing
the boy's tunic and lifting him to his shoulders. Taking a hand-
ful of ripe olives from the bowl, he filled his mouth as he told
Ireina of Sicarus's offer for her and Demos to live on his farm
while they were gone. Ireina gave a small frown of disappointment at the news but, as she always did, accepted whatever he
said without argument. If he said that he had to go to some place
called Carthage, wherever that was, he must have a good reason. The idea of living on a farm pleased her, and she knew that
Demos would like being around the animals.

The rest of the day they spent alone, each of them taking turns keeping Demos amused. It was good for him to watch Ireina and their child together. Casca reflected on their time together and how much of a child she still was. He loved her, but it was not in the way he'd loved Lida of Helsfjord those long years back. This was a different kind of love. In some ways it was similar to what he felt about Demos. The innocence and trust of the child was equaled in the mother. They both had a trusting faith that as long as he was near them, nothing could do them harm. To Ireina, he was still the sleeping warrior who had waited for her to awaken him. He was a fantasy character who had come true, and she was living the fantasy. If she had been able to put that away, he might have been able to love her in a different manner.

Now the best he could do was to make sure that she and Demos wouldn't be hurt and would have enough money to live on when he left them, as he knew he would have to do some day. The thought hurt, for he loved the boy and the boy's mother each in their own fashion. But the child would not stay small forever, and even Ireina must one day see, as her hair turned silver and her skin wrinkled, that he stayed the same. He would have to go before then, and he would need money to give her security, for she was not very wise in the ways of the outside world. Her life in the distant mountains was the only one she knew. She would never have the guile to make her way in the civilized world, where lies were more powerful than truth.

Well, that was in the future. For now, he was content just to enjoy having someone who cared for him. He would handle the rest of the problems as they came. As was the norm, they went to sleep with the setting of the sun; oil was still too expensive a luxury to waste on lamps. His internal clock woke him before dawn. He opened the shutters to their room to let in what light was available from the glow of the moon. By this, he prepared himself for departure. When he was ready, he woke Ireina and helped her gather their few belongings into a bundle as they waited for the slaves of Sicarus to come for her.

With the first light, he heard the clatter of a wagon on the street below. Wrapping Demos in a blanket, he carried the child down the stairs, with Ireina toting their bundles. She had said little about his leaving. She knew that he would return and that, as always, everything would be well. Demos snuggled his head closer to Casca's chest and mumbled in his sleep, never waking as he and his mother were put on the cart, Demos to lie on a bed of straw in the back and Ireina to sit next to an elderly house slave on the seat of the mule-drawn cart. A single rider was to escort them, a stern-faced man of nearly fifty with the marks of a warrior on him and eyes that did not turn away from a straight look. He was one of Sicarus's retired fighters who now lived at his farm. Ireina and Demos would be safe with him.

She leaned over for Casca to kiss her farewell. Childlike in her trust and love, she let her lips rest gently on the man from time. He touched the curls of Demos, gently marveling at the fine texture of the boy's hair. He hated to leave them. Turning quickly, he returned to the inn for his gear as the clatter of the wooden wheels of the cart faded on the cobblestones. He felt not only a little sadness at their leaving but also a sense of relief that now he would be free for a time from the responsibility of wife and son now that they were on their way to safety. He could now put his mind completely on the job at hand. If things went well on this operation, he could possibly make enough to buy them their own farm, in an area where wars seldom came and trouble was something that happened only to others.

There was dew on the stones from the mist that came in from the Bosphorus. As Casca walked to the piers, from either side of the street the sounds of people waking for the new day came to him. Mixed odors of cooking food and urine mingled with the salt of the mist and smoke from a hundred thousand small cooking fires. Soon the streets would begin to fill, men and slaves on their way to their jobs, to do the thousand things that made up a civilized metropolis. Sewer workers and stonemasons, whores and merchants, lawmakers and lawbreakers, soldiers and priests. As he neared the quays, he heard the racket of men already at work, loading ships to catch the morning tide out to sea. Horses whinnied and left droppings to mark their passage. Sea captains railed at their crews for being lazy swine as soldiers kept order with the threat of their lances.

A cheerful hail directed him to his destination. Hrolvath came bounding over to him, resembling, to Casca's mind, a young, playful, half-grown pup. Gods, does that boy never stop being happy? Who the hell can have that much energy this early in the morning? I must be getting old. The idea of his getting old tickled Casca a bit, and he laughed in spite of his earlier grumpiness.

Hrolvath met him, gushing with good humor. He took Casca's pack from him, ignoring any protests, and led him to the dock where their ship, an imperial trireme, was being loaded. Two other ships would make up their small flotilla, being used to transport their animals and most of the heavy equipment and food stores.

Sicarus was busy cursing a number of slaves who were having difficulties getting their horses loaded into the belly of a stout trader. He spotted Casca with Hrolvath and waved at him, asking if Ireina and Demos had been picked up on time. Once Casca had assured him that they were safely on their way to his farm, Sicarus told him to stay with Hrolvath, who knew what ship he was to be on. They would be loaded and ready to leave within the hour. Other mercenaries stood about in small groups, most of them looking a bit bewildered by all the confusion. Most had never left by sea for an action before, and many had never even been on a ship. Casca didn't envy them their first experience, especially if they ran into rough weather and felt their stomachs trying to crawl out of their mouths as their skins turned green.

Hrolvath led him to the trireme, saying, "Sicarus likes you a great deal and wants you with him where you can spend some time together. He wants to talk with you. That's a good sign. I think he's going to make you a squad leader. If he does, can I be in it?"

The eagerness in the boy's words were a novelty to Casca. He didn't know why Hrolvath had taken such a liking to him. But what the hell could it hurt? He did like the boy in spite of his unbridled energy and enthusiasm.

They found a perch on the bow above the bronze-plated battering ram that served as the prow of the vessel. From there, he could see Sicarus and the harbor master screaming invectives as each blamed the other for generally screwing up everything. Once that was done and each had satisfied his honor by casting every possible abuse and question about the other's parentage, things sorted themselves out. In an amazingly short time, Sicarus came on board the trireme and had a short conference with what was obviously the captain, a man wearing a plumed gilded helmet and rich armor embossed with the profiles of dolphins and Poseidon.

Soon the captain ordered the dock hands to cast off the mooring lines. Tow boats pulled the head of the large ship around to face the open sea and then moved off. The captain gave the command for his six hundred slaves to set oars on the mark of the hortator's drum. The first stroke of the sweeps was made, and they were free of the land. In front of them, the clear, glassy ocean waited, and beyond that the shores of north Africa and the ancient city of the sea kings of Phoenecia, home of the most dangerous threat to Rome, Carthage, now the capital of the empire of the Vandals, who had razed much of Europe on their way past the Pillars of Hercules to the shores of Africa, where they had built their new empire on the bones of the old.

CHAPTER EIGHT

Hrolvath

They were well away. Sails were set, the slave oars were shipped, and the drum of the hortator went silent. Sicarus sent for Casca and Hrolvath to come to his cabin on the upper deck.

Imperial marines kept watch not only on the open sea but also on the lower decks, where the oar slaves were chained to their rowing benches. Casca commiserated with them, recalling his long years on the benches of the warships of Rome. If the ship went down in battle, all the slaves would die, unable to free themselves from their chains. If they won and lived, there was only the prospect of a life of endless toil for most of them. Few ever lived to the end of their sentences.

Casca's reflections were interrupted by Hrolvath nudging his arm to bring him back to the present. Sicarus was speaking to them, inviting them to enter his cabin. Casca bent his head and entered the curtains to greet his leader. Hrolvath followed.

Sicarus indicated for them to take seats in the curule-shaped chairs of ebony set around a small round table inlaid with mother-of-pearl and ivory depicting scenes of the battle of Actium, where Pompey had defeated the forces of Antony and Cleopatra nearly five hundred years earlier.

Setting out a map scroll on the table, he told Casca and Hrolvath to attend his words. "I have invited you to join me, Casca, because I have long prided myself on being a good judge of both men and horses." He smiled as he continued. "Though I must admit that I have no more luck than anyone else where figuring out women is concerned."

Casca laughed appreciatively at the small joke. Hrolvath looked confused.

Pointing at Casca with a small straight dagger of Thracian design, he returned to business. "I believe that you have had experience and knowledge that I will need in the coming weeks. For that purpose, I ordered you assigned to this ship so that we may have an opportunity to get to know each other better. Then, if I am correct in my judgment, you may prove to be of great value to me and my brigade. Hrolvath is here because for some reason the boy has taken a great liking to you. Perhaps it is because you are the only one to ever get the best of him, even if it was by a trick." He turned the point of the dagger to the map on the table. "Now tell me, what do you think of the region to which we are going as a staging area?" He indicated the port of Tripoli, a thousand miles' distance across the Mediterranean, as their destination.

Casca thought a minute before asking, "Are we going straight across or do we make any stops along the way?"

Sicarus told him to say what he thought would be the best course of action.

Casca eyed the distance again before speaking. "As far as a staging area for an assault on Carthage, it's fine, as long as it's not too heavily defended. But I would recommend that we make the trip with two stops."

Sicarus prodded him. "Why?"

Casca grunted, knowing that Sicarus had probably already come to the same conclusion. The mercenary leader just wanted to hear him say the right words. "On a trip like this, with men who are not used to the sea and animals that have been confined for long periods, with water that can go bad and grain that will sour, we would have both men and animals in better shape if we made stops at Crete, then at either Cyrene or Berenice on the African coast for a couple of days before attempting a landing at Tripoli. In terms of time, it would not mean a loss of more than a few days, yet it could mean a difference in our combat capabilities if we meet the enemy on the beach."

Sicarus smiled, pleased at his analysis. The brute did have a brain above those large shoulders, and he knew how to use it. That was of more value to him than a dozen fighters. Men who could think in times of crisis were worth more than gold. They could, and often did, spell the difference between victory and disaster.

Pleased, he called for wine to be served and had the red and blue striped curtains surrounding his cabin raised fully to take best advantage of the breeze.

"That is exactly what we are going to do. Once we have reached Cyrene, a land force under Belisarius will already be ten days in front of us, going across land to assist us in reducing Tripoli. We are to land to the north of the city and set about generally making ourselves a nuisance, to draw off as many of the city forces as possible. Then, when Belisarius is ready, we will join him and put ourselves between whatever forces we have lured out of the walls and then eliminate them piecemeal before assaulting the walls. Belisarius should make good time, as we are carrying in the holds of our ships most of his heavy equipment, such as the ballistae and catapults."

Casca grunted in appreciation of the basic plan. He had heard much about Belisarius, but not from anyone who had served with him firsthand. He asked Sicarus what he knew of the man.

Sicarus was more than ready to give Casca the information. It was not that he was in the habit of blindly trusting anyone who came into his camp, but he did have the wife and child of the man at his home, in the event that he had made a bad judgment. They would make admirable hostages for Casca's good behavior.

Clearing his throat with a draught of tart Lesbos wine, he told Casca how he had first met Belisarius and the service he had rendered him and the Emperor Justinian I.

"Belisarius is the finest commander in the empire. When he was only twenty-five, he defeated the Persians at Darus, then returned to Constantinople for his victory. While there, the two major political factions, known as the blues and the greens, started a bunch of shit. The greens, also known as the Nikas, attempted a coup. The blues stayed on the fence, ready to go whichever way the wind blew. The greens had many followers among the common folk and in the army. Belisarius came to me for assistance, and I gave it. My mercenaries and few loyal units of the imperial guard were all that saved the throne for Justinian. Because of that service, my brigade of mercenaries has always been given preferential treatment and the choicest assignments. We do have some enemies at court, though, the most important of them being the eunuch faction headed by Gregory the officorum magister, who, in his position, has virtual control over who gets what office at court, and the soldier eunuch

Narses, who is very tight with Gregory and shows him a great deal of deference. I must confess, Narses is a very capable commander, but there is something about men who voluntarily have their balls cut off that puts me a little bit ill at ease around them.''

Hrolvath asked him to talk about the eunuch general a bit more. Sicarus wetted his whistle with another draught before proceeding. ''Narses was born in Persarmenia. He is a small, well-formed man, not fat like most eunuchs but still given to fine dress and exquisite manners. Currently, he holds the position of sacellarius, by which he commands a bodyguard detachment of eunuchs who stay close to the person of the emperor. To my way of thinking, that is not a good thing. I hate to admit it, but he was instrumental in bringing the blues over to the imperial side through the judicious use of extravagant bribes and payoffs. They did aid somewhat in keeping many people out of the revolt.''

Casca queried him about the reason for eunuchs being in such positions of power and trust in the court. Sicarus tried to explain the thinking process behind it. ''The court believes that men who have no balls have no ambition and can therefore be trusted more than normal men.''

Casca snorted. ''Bullshit! With no balls, what do they have left to entertain themselves with, except for intrigue and plots of one kind or another? I've found that no matter what the reason they were cut, they all have a hatred for those who still have their gonads intact.''

Sicarus was in complete agreement with Casca. Hrolvath said little, not really having much experience with such people or matters. He was content to sit and listen.

Sicarus let them go to their quarters, which was no more than a small place where they were able to string up a hammock near the bow. It was the roughest part of the ship to ride in and, because of that, the least popular as a place to sleep, leaving them more room than the others had in exchange for their discomfort.

During the next days, as they wove their way through the rocky islands of the Cyclades, Casca had a lot of free time with which to get to know Hrolvath better. Much of this time they spent fencing. Casca was naturally very interested in this new technique of swordplay.

''Hrolvath, how did you come to develop your style and weapon?''

Resting the point of his long sword between his feet as they stood on the deck of the galley watching the waves rise and fall in front of them, Hrolvath smiled shyly as he explained. "My father was a sword master for the governor of the diocese of Dacia and in charge of teaching the children of several noble houses the art of swordplay. As a child I was not very strong, but my reflexes were quick. Often I was picked on by other children who were larger and stronger. I couldn't compete with them on their level by using the heavy short or long swords. But as I watched, it always appeared that they were open to long straight thrusts, and the heavier swords made their counters seem terribly slow and awkward."

Hrolvath made a couple of passes at the wind with his sword to emphasize his words.

"During one of these times, one of the older boys was picking on me as I watched them spar. He began to call me a girl and fit only for sweeping up kitchens. Then he tossed a broken broom at me, which I caught, and without thinking, I took a swipe at him. My father was watching me, though I didn't know it, and when the bully blocked my attack and came at me with his short sword, it was more luck than thought that I was able to parry his blade with the end of the broom. Then, when he made a lunge, I just straightened my arm out. With the extra length of the handle and my extended arm, the broom simply slid over his guard, and he ran onto the blunted end, nearly breaking his neck.

"At that point, my father broke up what was going to be a severe beating for me by the boys for hurting their friend with my unfair use of the broom handle. From then on, my father began to experiment with longer, thinner swords.

"He had several different types made by the governor's smithy. We would spend hours testing them against other swords and even short spears and pikes. Not everyone has the strength to wave around one of those heavy blades such as yours for hours. For such as myself, this was the perfect weapon. By using its length and suppleness, I was able to spar for long periods without tiring, while my heavier opponents worked themselves into a state of exhaustion. Then it was an easy matter to just reach out and pin them where I chose. My father tried to interest others in the style, but to no avail. They were just not interested in anything new. So he concentrated his efforts on me. At least I would be able to protect myself when he wasn't around anymore, and even though our new style was scoffed at by everyone, it didn't take many times before the other boys chose to leave me alone and no longer challenge me to duels. They would curse me for being a coward and not fighting the normal way that gentlemen should, but they still kept their distance, and that was all I wanted from them.''

Casca was impressed at what the boy and his father had developed. It was something that could revolutionize sword work if it caught on.

Hrolvath tried to show him some of the basic moves and techniques of the new thin, long sword. At first Casca thought it awkward and not very effective for him. He was used to the heavier, more comfortable weight of a blade that could smash through a stout iron helmet or slice through a breastplate of steel scales. Hrolvath changed his mind. He demonstrated that instead of having to use force to crash through the helmet, with the thin longer point he could go into the open eye sockets of a helmet or reach the throat while staying out of the range of his enemy. The chest was not as vulnerable, but there were always chinks in armor. When an arm was raised, the armpit was exposed, and a long thrust could penetrate straight to the heart or lungs. Then there was the junction between neck and head, which always provided a good target for a lightning-quick thrust. The greatest weakness of the sword was shown when an opponent managed to get in close under the weapon or a good strong counterblow below the midway point of the long thin blade caused it to snap. Because of that, Hrolvath said, he always carried at least two of the long swords with him in battle.

It took a little time, but in a few days Casca began to feel more comfortable with the new sword, though he felt he would never have the suppleness of wrist that Hrolvath had. It reminded him in some ways of the open-hand techniques of fighting he had seen while in the lands of China, beyond the great wall, where he had served in the army of the eastern emperor, Tzin. There too they emphasized not brute force but balance and style, to use the least amount of force necessary to achieve your purpose, whether it was to merely disable or to kill. Never to use force or energy that wasn't required. The sword of Hrolvath was much like that.

It was a good time for Casca and Hrolvath. They found that each had many qualities that the other liked. Hrolvath was a completely guileless lad who was doing his best to live what he thought of as a romantic adventure. He had blind faith and trust in Sicarus. He knew that if the mercenary leader took on a contract, he did it for the right reasons, not just for loot or the pleasure of killing. In his way Sicarus was a dreamer, too, a throwback to the times when men fought for what they believed was their honor. He had found his counterpart in Belisarius, and as Hrolvath was devoted to him, so he was to Belisarius.

Casca looked forward to meeting the man. From all that he had heard of him, he was the best that the Eastern or Western empires had to offer against the barbarians of the north and west and the Persians of the Sassanian Empire. When he took the field, it was with pathetically small forces, considering the population of Byzantium. From a population of over thirty million, he was seldom given more than thirty thousand regular soldiers. He had to flesh out his forces by hiring local auxiliaries and some mercenary units, such as those of Sicarus. But the heart of his army was the regular soldiers and his heavy cavalry, for which a new breed of horse had been bred that could carry the heavily armored knights with relative ease.

He had his own special force, known as the commander's bodyguard, consisting of fifteen hundred highly trained and motivated light cavalrymen. For sieges, he relied on the sophisticated weapons of the royal arsenal, the ballistae and catapults, which could toss pots of the famous Greek fire over the highest of walls to set the inside of a city on fire. His forces may have been small, but they were all motivated by his personal example of leadership and courage. Hearing this, Casca thought that he was much like the Roman commanders of old, including the great Julius, who never hesitated to share the hardships of common foot soldiers or the danger. And by this, their men came to love them to such a degree that they could never conceive of letting their leaders down by failing to complete their missions, even if it meant death.

Twice on the sail through the Cyclades Casca saw what he thought were the black lateen sails of island pirates, but they kept their distance from the heavy galley and its escort. They would go on to find more vulnerable prey.

The weather stayed good, with only a few swells of fifteen or twenty feet at times when the winds rose. This was enough, however, to send several hundred otherwise courageous mercenaries to the railings, where they emptied their stomachs into the deep, along with their bravery, as most of them begged for mercy from the sea gods, forgetting for a moment their new Christian ethics. Hrolvath never seemed to be affected by anything. He grew golden-skinned from the warm sun of the Mediterranean and relished each new day that brought them closer to the shores of Africa, where he would at last face his first real battle. He had participated in several smaller actions in the service of Sicarus, but that was mostly chasing Armenian bandits back into their mountainous strongholds until winter sealed them in for another season. This was to be a battle against the Vandals who had ravaged most of Europe and defeated a dozen Roman armies in open battle.

There was a short stop at Crete for resupplying and to let the men stretch their legs for a day on solid ground. The horses were kept on board. It would have been too much of a delay to offload them for such a short time. Three of the horses had died from unknown causes, and their carcasses were tossed over the side, where in seconds schools of dorsal fins gathered about them to feed, turning the waters into small whirlpools of red froth. The sharks' feeding made several of the tough warriors a bit ill. There was something terribly frightening, almost indecent, about the idea of being eaten by those saber-toothed fish whose jaws ripped the large war-horses into bloody shreds in minutes.

From Crete, they had a clear run to Cyrene, six hundred miles west of Alexandria and nearly the same distance from Carthage.

Facing to the wind, Casca thought he could smell the dry winds of the desert riding over the waters of the sea. Soon they would be at Cyrene, and then he would have a chance to see for himself what Belisarius was like. Sicarus had promised him they would meet.

CHAPTER NINE

Pompeianus

They were on the last leg of the trip to Cyrene. Fair winds made the use of oars minimal for a few days, but Casca knew that it was hell below the decks, where little or no breeze came through to ease the stifling heat. There, in the semidarkness, he could feel the men sweating, unable to move more than a few inches at a time, the chains cutting into their flesh, leaving ulcers on the ankles that would never heal. The flesh of the buttocks did one of two things. Either it grew hard as boiled leather and calloused or it developed sores that ate away the tissue till the suppurating holes reached the bone. Usually death followed not long after that, either from disease entering through the sores or because the slaves were no longer able to pull strongly enough at the sweeps and therefore became expendable.

Sometimes the coughing sickness would sweep through the entire lower decks, killing men by twos and threes till there was no one left to man the oars, and the regular crewmen and marines had to sit on the benches and get a taste of having to manhandle the thirty-foot sweeps in unison for hours at a time, till the flesh peeled from their hands and their blood joined that of the hundreds of condemned men who had sat on the benches before them. It gave them a small taste of hell, and few who ever sat on those benches ever treated oar slaves with quite the same contempt again; they had tasted their pain, if only for a short time.

Casca moved down the steps leading to the slave benches. He had tried to stay away but was drawn to them for some reason he didn't want to examine too closely.

The smell of packed humanity swept over him. The myriad odors of hundreds of unwashed bodies mingled with the stale acrid stench of urine from the pots beneath the benches. There the men ate, slept, pissed, shit, and died, never leaving those benches till the day they were freed or thrown over the side.

On the slave benches, there were no prejudices shown. Arabs, Jews, Syrians, Persian, Armenians, Goths, Vandals, Greeks, Romans, thieves, pimps, murderers, tax evaders, and those convicted of heresy all shared the same destiny.

Several guards stood at either end of the walkway separating the two banks of oarsmen that ran the length of the galley. The heat made them sluggish, semidrugged from the heaviness of the air inside. Even with the ports open, little breeze could find its way into the floating dungeon. To guard the slaves was a dehumanizing experience. The only way to keep one's sanity was to not think of them as men; they were, instead, machines of bone and flesh that existed only to serve the ship by pulling the oars.

Casca found a seat on the stairs near the stern end of the walkway, near the drum of the hortator, which was now idle. He could feel in his bones the beat that set the mark and tempo of the slaves' efforts. When the beat was set to half stroke, it wasn't too bad. You could get lost in the rhythm of movement. Even full stroke could be endured for a time before arms and backs began to break under the strain, but there was nothing like the hellish drive of ramming speed to break a man. It was nearly impossible for anyone to keep up the measure for more than twenty minutes. During those twenty minutes, men would die on the benches, their open mouths spouting bright red blood from ruptured hearts. Others would collapse over their oars in uncontrollable muscle spasms, with tendons and ligaments torn free from their anchors. Even the whips couldn't penetrate through the red glazé that consumed one's mind in those horrible minutes.

He had seen men who had to be killed to stop them from rowing. When they would no longer respond to command, they had become lost in the mad rhythm of the drum beat. Their souls had become one with the oars and the cycles of pulling the handle of the sweeps to the chest, right foot set on the block under the benches in front of them to give the rowers more strength.

Pull to the chest, leaning back as far as you could, then a half circle down on the handles to raise the blades from the water, a shove forward to prepare them to be set again, then a precious moment's rest as the weight of the oars was released for the space of a heartbeat to fall back into the waters before the cycle was repeated. The pattern never changed, and they became trapped in that pattern and couldn't stop of their own accord. They would row until their hearts burst or a thrust from a guard's lance ended their labors.

Then the useless husk would be tossed to the sharks and one of the spare rowers would be brought up from the holds to take the empty seat. Every good ship always carried a supply of spare rowers.

A scream pierced through the fog of Casca's recollections, jerking him back to the present, hand on sword. A slave had broken free from his chains, as sometimes happened when the wood became rotten or the bolts rusted through beneath the surface of the wood, where it couldn't be detected by the oar master. Reflex made Casca draw his sword as the hysterical slave raced at him, chains dragging at his feet, eyes wild, mouth flecked with the foam of madness. He screamed and screamed again, blindly running the length of the walkway. One of the guards tried a cast with his javelin and missed his target, pinning another slave to the deck.

The screaming man ran straight into Casca, stopping only when Casca held him to his chest with his left arm around the wretch's ulcerous shoulders. The man looked at him, tears running from his eyes as he cried through a mouth from which the teeth had long ago fallen out.

Sobbing, the man cried out, "Don't let them take me back. Don't let them take me back. I would rather die!"

Casca tensed his left arm, holding the man firmly to his chest. Placing the point of his sword onto the space in the upper chest where the heart lay, he shoved the point in quickly, giving the man peace. As he let the body slide down to the planks, he spoke so softly that no one else could have heard:

"I understand. There are things in life many times more terrible than death. I give you your escape."

As the guards approached him, they congratulated him on his quick actions. They would have been in a lot of trouble if the slave had reached the upper decks and disturbed the captain. Casca was tempted for a moment to strike out at them. But to what purpose? They were only doing their job, and it would not have helped the other slaves. He had responsibilities now; he had to think of Ireina and Demos. He would do nothing that would have him put in chains, unable to return to them.

Feeling depressed, he returned to the upper decks, found a leather bucket, and threw it over the side, hauling up some clean water to wash away the slave's blood. Hrolvath came running to him, asking if he was all right, saying that he'd heard that Casca had been attacked by a slave who'd run amok and had tried to kill him.

Casca shook his head a bit angrily. "He wasn't trying to attack me. I merely helped him find that which he was seeking."

Hrolvath didn't understand what Casca meant by that, but he could hear the sadness in the tones of the Roman's words and knew that what had happened had brought a great sadness to his friend.

It was the next morning when Sicarus called the two to him on the bow. He pointed to a dark line on the horizon. "Cyrene lies there. We will make port in a few hours. This will be our last stop before Tripoli. Here we should have our next orders waiting for us from Belisarius. Then, if things have not changed, we'll sail in two days to our rendezvous point."

With the wind behind them, they were able to sail into the harbor entrance nearly to the piers before the sails were dropped and the oars set out to guide them the last few yards to where lines were tossed out for slaves to haul them into the side of the stone wharf and gently come to rest.

Sicarus, escorted by Casca and Hrolvath, was the first to leave the pier, to be met by a centurion, who was the emissary of Belisarius. The officer led them into the town, which to Casca looked much like all the others of the African and the Mediterranean coastal region. Flat-roofed, whitewashed one- and two-storied structures made of either stone or sun-baked bricks of mud, except that it had more of the Egyptian touch to many of its public buildings, which were leftovers from the times of the pharaohs. In the center of the city, near the public offices, were several large obelisks, set there to commemorate the passage of some pharaoh's army to do battle with tribes now long forgotten. Only the huge monoliths remained to mark the passing of an empire that had equaled and surpassed many of the accomplishments of Rome in its prime.

There was harshness to the glare of the sun that pierced the eyes, evidence that not far beyond the green fringe of the coast, the trackless wastes of the desert lay as they had for eons. A host only to the few nomads who had learned to live in harmony with the great wastelands that were friends only to the lizard and the sand viper.

Inside the welcome shade of the headquarters for the local garrison, Sicarus was greeted by the praetor, Cornelius Pompeianus, the city commander, a member of the Illustrii. Distaste at having to have any dialogue with one of such disreputable origins was written clearly on his patrician face. He didn't give in to bad manners, though, and forced himself to offer at least the barest minimum of courtesies by indicating for his guests to have a seat.

Sicarus knew the type, and it didn't bother him at all. He knew that these pompous smug asses would put on their airs of superiority because of some accident of birth and then cry for his help when they couldn't handle things themselves. They would say that he was the best of friends, until such time as he had done all the dirty work for them and would once more be relegated to the status of a lesser being.

Pompeianus looked with even greater distaste at the overmuscled, scar-faced scoundrel who was scowling at him over Sicarus's shoulder. He was most definitely a brute of a lower order. But the young man with the gold hair and fine glowing skin seemed to be several cuts above his companions. He thought he even detected a certain sensitivity in the curve of the lips. Yes, a most interesting young man, one who might not be averse to having his status in life improved through the efforts of a gracious and understanding sponsor.

It was with reluctance that he returned his attention to the business at hand. Putting on the best face he could, he handed over the sealed written orders left in his care by Belisarius, who was now ten days' march somewhere along the coast. Cornelius felt slighted that he was privy to the contents of the letter or even the eventual destination of Belisarius and his forces. Why were these mercenaries in his district? He didn't think they would be going to battle the Vandals. That was too horrible to think of. It had been many years since the army had taken the field against the barbarians, and then it had not gone well.

No! It had something to do with Justinian's constant harping about opening up new trade routes to the distant East. This was most likely just a strong scouting force to determine what resistance might be found among the tribesmen and savages of the deserts. If there had been any thoughts of war, surely he would have been informed, as his jurisdiction lay on the most direct route to the Vandal domain and the same path they would take if they decided to move against Egypt.

Sicarus removed himself to where the light was a bit better to open the sealed letter from Belisarius and also to keep Cornelius from seeing anything.

Inside were his next instructions and a written order for the garrison commander to give the mercenaries whatever they wanted in terms of supplies. This had been anticipated by Sicarus, who had his list of demands ready. These he handed over to Cornelius, along with the order written in Belisarius's own hand, commanding him to put himself and his warehouses at the disposal of Sicarus.

Cornelius wished there had been some way to refuse the demands made on his resources. If he gave the mercenaries all they wanted, his own storehouse would barely be able to handle his requirements till the next harvest. Why did they need so much grain? Were they going to trade it to the desert savages for ivory or gold? That wasn't a bad idea. The nomads were always hungry. Perhaps he would be able to mount a small expedition of his own later, using what he normally skimmed from the harvest.

Turning on the charm, he escorted his guests to the door, promising to see to their requests with all possible dispatch. He managed to separate Hrolvath from the others for a moment and whispered in the boy's ear for him to come to his quarters on the hill near the east wall after sunset. He had something of importance to say to him which could have an effect upon him and his comrades. Conspiratorialy, he touched the side of his nose to indicate secrecy in the matter. Hrolvath didn't know what to make of it, but if the man had any information to give him, he would have to go.

They returned to the galley, finding that most of their men had offloaded and were already well established in the waterfront taverns. Sicarus didn't mind too much. They needed something to ease the wobbles from their legs and had to give vent to their emotions.

In each of the taverns there were at least two of his mercenary squad leaders, with a couple of others who didn't take part in the drinking. They were there to make certain that all the men got safely back to the ships on time and to ascertain that they didn't make too much trouble among the locals. The next day they would have their chance to party, and others would watch over them. No man was permitted outside the waterfront on pain of flogging unless he had express permission from Sicarus.

Casca was sent on various errands for Sicarus, as was Hrolvath. Sicarus stayed close to the ship so that he could be located easily if anyone had problems. It wasn't before midday before the first of his warriors began to return, most not under their own power. These were hauled aboard with no ceremony and moved down to the holds of whichever ship they belonged to by the squad leaders, who then returned to gather more of their besotted comrades.

Near sundown, Casca returned for his last errand and asked where Hrolvath was. Sicarus responded that he hadn't seen him for about an hour but that he should be coming back any time. Things eased off a bit, and they were able to sit down and take a break, enjoying the cool breeze coming in from the sea with the night.

Sicarus had a pot of Egyptian beer brought to him from one of the taverns. It was a bit yeasty and smelled of fermented dates, but all in all it wasn't too bad. Casca had drunk better and worse in his time. During the conversation, the talk got around to Hrolvath.

Casca asked between swallows, "Why do you keep Hrolvath with you, and why do you use him to test newcomers?"

Sicarus smiled gently. "I like the boy for one thing. He is always good-natured, and his courage has never been lacking when things got tight. Why do I use him to test volunteers? You yourself have seen how he can handle that sword of his. The rest of the men feel the same as I do. He's more of a mascot to bring them luck. I have had a problem a couple of times keeping some of those who would use him like woman in their place. But once they understood that the penalty for taking a free man or woman against his will was death, they left him alone. I know that he looks, and even moves, a bit like a young girl, but he has not as of yet shown any interest in anyone of either sex. I think he is exactly what he appears to be: a young man of great beauty and courage who lives a bit in a fantasy world."

Casca had to agree with Sicarus's analysis of Hrolvath. He was getting a bit concerned about where the boy was. He, too, was developing the same protective attitude that most of the other mercenaries felt toward the lad.

Sicarus ordered one of his squad leaders to go look for him, saying that the last place he had been sent was the warehouse to see if a shipment of spears and arrowheads was ready to be loaded.

It was full dark by the time the squad leader reported, slapping his fist against his chest in salute. "Sir, Hrolvath is not on the waterfront. The last anyone saw of him, he was heading to inner city."

Sicarus's brow wrinkled in concern as he turned to Casca. "Did he say anything to you about going into town?"

Casca shook his head. "Not a word." He thought a bit and then asked Sicarus, "Did he say what it was that Pompeianus spoke to him of?"

Sicarus said with certainty, "No! I wasn't aware they had even spoken together. Why?"

Casca shook his head. "I don't know, but before we left the garrison headquarters, I saw Pompeianus pull him over to the side and talk with him for a moment. I thought perhaps the praetor had a message to give you that he didn't want me to hear."

The squad leader cleared his throat to attract his leader's attention.

"Do you have something you wish to say?" Sicarus demanded.

The man cleared his throat again, thinking how best to phrase his thoughts. It wasn't normally very wise to say anything about your social betters, but then, he had been asked. "Sir, I don't know for sure. It may only be waterfront bullshit, but . . ."

Sicarus rose from his chair, seeming a bit pissed. "But what, you ape? If you've heard something, then out with it, and now!"

Taking on a wounded look, the man finished his story: "It has been said by several of the soldiers stationed here that the easiest way to a promotion is through the bedroom of the garrison commander, especially if you're a young pretty boy."

Sicarus's face clouded. "He wouldn't dare leave the docks without my permission. He knows that my rules apply to everyone. I don't care how much I like him, I will not tolerate willful disobedience." He was working himself into a rage.

Casca tried to cool him off a bit, saying gently, "Take it easy. You know Hrolvath too well to think he would just take off for a rendezvous with a puffy pervert. If he's gone to Pompeianus, there has to be a good reason for it."

At that thought, Sicarus was ready to call out his men, arm them, and storm the city if need be to get his man back. Casca cooled him down again.

"Why don't you just let me go in and look for him? Remember, there's still a contract to be fulfilled. You don't want to screw things up right now. You would fail in your word to Belisarius."

With some reluctance Sicarus agreed to Casca's plan but warned him that if he failed, the mercenaries would feed the praetor's body to the seagulls an inch at a time, contract or no contract. His first obligation was to the men who served under his command, and they would never be able to say that he had deserted any one of them for any reason.

Casca returned to the galley just long enough to arm himself with a breastplate, which he concealed under his tunic of gray homespun, and his sword. Heading back into the inner city, he stopped to ask a member of the vigeles patrolling the waterfront where the house of the praetor Pompeianus was. He received his directions, with the warning not to turn his back on the praetor if he valued the ability to sit down without pain, for the praetor's favorite move with his personal weapons was the butt stroke.

With that bit of humor, Casca picked up his pace to just short of running.

CHAPTER TEN

Cornelius Pompeianus, praetor of Cyrene, had spent the rest of the day after the mercenaries left preparing for his meeting with the young savage. After his bath, he had his body slaves perfume his body and curl his hair, scenting it delicately with precious oils. The quality of his household slaves had been remarked on often by men of taste. He took great pride in them. All were young males whom he had selected himself and had personally trained in their duties. Men were so much more conscientious than females.

He had learned how to initiate them into his lifestyle by using a variety of techniques, and most had been grateful to him for the new awareness he had brought into their lives. True, there had been a few who were incorrigible, and those had had to be disposed of. It would not do to have slaves who had once been close to his person living in another household where they could speak ill of him.

For his wardrobe, he selected a knee-length, loose-flowing tunic of emerald with traces of gold thread woven into the fabric.

Once his toilet was complete, he admired the results in a mirror of rare Persian glass. The results pleased him. He looked, in his eyes, to be noble yet understanding, a soldier who had known battle but had not lost his sensitivity.

He hoped the boy wouldn't be a disappointment, as had been the case too many times in the past. Sighing, he reclined on a couch of Greek fashion in his garden to wait for the golden child to appear. He closed his eyes to let his imagination add spice to the adventure he was planning. He knew that the boy would be grateful to him after he had initiated him into the pleasures that only one man can truly give to another. Not the shallow sweating and grunting of women, who had no true understanding of a man's needs. They were fit only for the rearing of children; after that they served no real purpose.

The Greeks, whom he greatly admired, had proved the value of love between men, even going into battle with their lovers as shield mates. It thrilled him to think of the glory of standing side by side with one you loved in the heat of battle. If his lover fell, he would wreak terrible vengeance upon those who had killed the boy. He would fight like a demon, a man possessed taking vengeance for the beauty the enemy had taken from his life. The beauty and tenderness of the thought brought a single tear to the corner of his eye, which he delicately removed with a silk kerchief.

He called for wine to be brought and spring water with which to cut it. Cloves were set by the tray to freshen the mouth. It wouldn't be much longer. He shivered with anticipated pleasure, recalling the manner in which the cheeks of Hrolvath's butt moved with such firmness when the boy walked, the manner in which he held his head, so straight and proud, the golden hair and the lips which he was certain were full of sleeping passions, waiting only for the right teacher to awaken them to their full glory.

What was taking the boy so long? It was already dark. The sun had set in the sea over half an hour ago. Perhaps the boy saw my desire and wishes to tease me a bit, to make me worry so that I will appreciate him even more when he does appear, he thought. He drank half a glass of wine without cutting it with water, not displeased at the idea.

He heard the rapping of the bronze knocker on his gate. A shiver ran over his thighs. He was here! Rising from his couch, he rearranged the wine bottles, taking care to set the one of Falernian near where he would have Hrolvath seated, just in case the boy was a bit shy or recalcitrant.

Hrolvath was shown into his presence by a Nubian servant who gave Hrolvath a dirty look when he was dismissed from his master's presence, leaving the two alone.

Cornelius walked rapidly across the garden to greet his guest, wrinkling his nose a bit as he neared. The boy smelled of sweat and salt air. He could fix that later; first things first.

"It is so good of you to come, young man. Now sit and take some wine. You look to be a bit dry from your day's labors."

Hrolvath refused the wine, saying, "I have to return to my

ship soon. What is the warning you have to give me for Sicarus?''

Cornelius smirked inwardly. So that was it! The boy admired his commander. A father figure perhaps, or was it that the child admired those of a martial nature? If that was the case, he could play the game as well as the vulgar mercenary.

''There is no need for us to rush. I will tell you everything in a few minutes. But please at least permit me to be a decent host.'' It was time to be careful. He would have to guide Hrolvath carefully.

Hrolvath was too well mannered to refuse the offer of hospitality. ''As you wish, sir, but I am in a hurry. My comrades will be wondering where I am.''

That pleased Cornelius. The boy had told no one where he was going. In that case, if things did not go well, the boy could just disappear, and none would be the wiser. His slaves would never speak, for they had been involved themselves in such a circumstance more than once. If he was questioned, he would claim ignorance of the boy's whereabouts. But he would naturally offer every aid to their search. That could only last, at most, two days, and then they would have to take ship. After that, there would be no more inquiries.

Cornelius led Hrolvath back to the garden, where the scent of night-blooming flowers sweetened the desert air. There he sat heavily on the cushions of his divan, showing the world-weary aspect of a man who has been beset with great responsibilities and has done his best to live up to them, even though his efforts have never been truly appreciated. Hrolvath was sympathetic and couldn't refuse the glass of wine offered him in the spirit of comradeship.

Cornelius poured him a draught of the Falernian in a goblet of cut crystal. He knew the way to break down the barriers to his desires. The wine had an additional spice in it that had never failed him. It would not make the young man completely unconscious, but it would reduce him to a state in which he would not be able to resist that which Cornelius wished to do with him. The only bad side effect was that Hrolvath would not be able to be fully involved with the pleasures that were planned for him, but he would make it up to the boy later.

Hrolvath tried to get Cornelius to tell what he had summoned him for, but it was so difficult to form the words. A strange heated flush ran over him, settling into his head. His arms and legs felt heavy, distant from the rest of his body. He couldn't move them properly. He tried to apologize for the wine he spilled when the glass fell from his loose fingers, but his tongue couldn't form the words.

Cornelius called for his servant to assist him. The Nubian and a dusky seventeen-year-old boy of indeterminate origins responded to their master's commands. In his stupor, Hrolvath was stripped naked and then bathed. His body was anointed with perfumes and oils. Soft silks of many colors were draped around his loins to add a bit of color and spice. Cornelius decided to be generous when he saw the pouting lips of his two body servants. He would permit them to join him in the initiation of Hrolvath to their little world of pleasures. Carefully, they strapped Hrolvath's wrists to the head of the couch on which they had laid him on his belly. Then his ankles were tied with strips of soft leather to the legs of the couch in order to keep them apart.

Cornelius was pleased; there was something tremendously exciting about having the fate of the beautiful boy in his hands. He could take him, use him, love him, or kill him. It really didn't matter which he did as long as it satisfied the need that ate at his soul, the need to be fulfilled. In this moment, he had the power of a god over the sweet flesh waiting for him. He removed his own robe, exposing his soft, fleshy body to the new moon rising over the walls of his garden.

The time was growing near. Soon Hrolvath would be nearly completely out of his drugged stupor. That was when he would take him. He would be first, and then he would permit the others to enjoy the golden body of the youth as he watched and renewed his strength and vitality. Hrolvath began to moan softly, shaking his head from side to side, trying to get some control over the whirlpool that was his mind and body. In a haze of twisting forms, the naked bodies of Cornelius and his servants swam in and out.

Cornelius was about ready. The passion, building to a crescendo in his loins, threatened to set his entire being on fire if he didn't quench the flames in the body of the helpless boy before him. Gods, it was fantastic to have such power! Cornelius prepared to lower his body over the back of Hrolvath.

"What the shit do you think you're doing?"

Cornelius jerked back at the interruption. The sight of the ugly brute with the sword in his hand caused his swollen manhood to shrink and become flaccid, the better to retreat back up into his groin, seeking shelter.

Casca had come over the garden wall. It took a second for him to realize what was going on. Then it hit him. Cornelius was going to rape the boy.

Cornelius put on an air of indignation. ''What do you think you are doing invading the privacy of my home? Don't you know that I can have you imprisoned or put to death?''

Casca snarled as he walked nearer them, his knuckles tightening on the grip of his sword. The two house slaves cowered behind Cornelius.

''I don't think you are going to do anything to anyone, you slime ball.'' He placed the point of his sword against Cornelius's Adam's apple. ''Do you think you can take one of ours and get away with it? If you had hurt Hrolvath, there would have been no way to keep Sicarus and his mercenaries from pulling this house down around your ears and feeding you your balls one at a time.''

Looking down at Hrolvath, lying there naked, his butt exposed to the night breeze, he turned on Cornelius. ''You seem to have a thing for bare fannys.'' He sliced the cords restraining Hrolvath, setting him free. Cornelius started to move away but was halted by the return of the point to his throat.

Hrolvath slid off the couch, groggily getting to his feet. He had to lean against a pillar to support his weight, shaking his head to clear the last of the mist from his mind.

Casca turned his attention to the two slaves, who were still cowering behind their master. ''Tie the praetor up the same way he had Hrolvath,'' he commanded. They hesitated till he laid the cheek of the seventeen-year-old open to the bone. ''I mean now.''

He jerked Cornelius by his hair, dragging him over to the couch on his stomach. A slap with the flat of his blade across the back served to keep the praetor from getting back up. Casca pointed to the cords. The slaves anxiously did his bidding, tying their master to the couch, afraid of what they were being forced to do but more afraid not to do it.

Once they had finished, he froze them in their steps by glaring at them, growling, ''Don't you move a muscle, or I'll split you open like ripe melons!''

They believed him. The whites of their eyes were wide with fright, and they kept their feet firmly in place as he moved around the garden till Casca found what he was looking for, some nice green saplings, half the thickness of his wrist. With a single sweep, he cut two of them and stripped them of their branches. These he put in the hands of the two slaves. Then he walked around in front of Cornelius, whose head was dangling over the edge of the couch. Casca took one of Cornelius's silk kerchiefs and stuffed it in the praetor's mouth. "I wouldn't want you to upset the neighbors," he commented. The slaves he placed near the head of Cornelius, facing his rear, the thick switches in their hands.

Casca ordered them to strike the buttocks of their master. When they hesitated, a gentle prod from the point of his sword provided them with all the impetus they needed. The thick switches sliced through the air, striking the exposed pale flesh. Another gentle prod and they repeated the process. Casca told them to keep it up till he gave them permission to stop. If they turned to speak, he would slice their throats. The slaves obeyed; in fact, they began to enjoy being the ones who did the beating for a change. It was thrilling to have the master under their power, to watch him jerk and twitch in pain.

Casca could see that they were getting into what they were doing. It was time to take Hrolvath and leave, after he performed one more chore. He raised Cornelius by the hair till the neck was extended, the tendons raised under the strain. Casca could see that the eyes were getting glazed. He wondered if it was from pain, or was the praetor getting off on pain? He hoped he was. Taking his small knife from his belt, he set the point gently against the side of the throat. Then, with the certainty of a surgeon, he pressed the point in, opening up small hole in the carotid artery. It was just large enough to permit each beat of the heart to send out a thin red spurt.

He set Cornelius's head back down. The sound of the open artery couldn't be heard, but Cornelius knew that he was going to die. He tried to drum his feet against the end of the table. His actions excited his slaves, who obeyed their orders from Casca with renewed vigor, applying the switches till the skin of Cornelius's ass blistered red, swelling till the skin was near the bursting point.

Casca gathered Hrolvath's things and took him by the arm to lend support as he gave a last warning to the slaves. "I'm going to sit down over here by the wall and watch. The first one of you who stops or turns to look at me dies. Is that understood?"

The anxious bobbing of heads confirmed that they did understand.

Casca took Hrolvath from the house, walking alongside the garden wall. He could hear the rhythm of the switches striking the skin of Cornelius, whose life blood was pumping from the hole in his neck. Hrolvath was getting his legs back. Casca helped him get dressed and then led him down the street toward the docks. Near a wine shop, he saw a couple of the city vigiles standing idly by.

As they neared, he called out to them: "Hey! I heard a cry near the house with the big wall around it. Sounded like someone being killed. I heard a couple of voices saying they were getting even with their master for something or other. Maybe you should check it out!" Casca gave them a bit more incentive to do so. "I'll inquire tomorrow with your centurion to see what it was all about."

The vigiles knew what house the scar-faced man was speaking of. They didn't really want to go there. More than once, screams had come from that house. As it belonged to their superior, they had made a point of ignoring anything that came from behind those walls. But if what the man had said was true, there might be trouble with the slaves. If they didn't check it out, what would they say to their commander in the morning when the scarface asked him about the incident? There were no options; they had to go see what was happening.

By the time Casca and Hrolvath reached the entrance to the port, Hrolvath was in full control of his faculties again. He told Casca how he had been lured to the home of the praetor and had to be stopped from making an embarrassing outburst of emotion to Casca for saving him.

They were met on the docks by Sicarus and three fully armed and armored mercenary squad leaders. It seemed that if Casca hadn't returned within a few more minutes, Sicarus and his entire force were prepared to go after them.

When he began to question Casca about the events of the evening, Hrolvath gave Casca a pleading look not to disgrace him in front of his comrades and leader. Casca simply shrugged it off and said that Hrolvath had been drugged by someone who said he had information for Sicarus. But he'd taken the boy back before any real harm could be done to him. It was close enough to the truth, and it got Hrolvath off the hook for leaving the dock without permission.

Sicarus knew that there was more to the story than that, but he was wise enough not to push it any further. He dismissed the squad leaders, sending them back to their men to spread the word that everything was all right.

Hrolvath, he told to go to his bunk; they would speak in the morning. Hrolvath touched Casca's arm in gratitude as he left to obey. Once they were alone, Sicarus tried to get Casca to tell all the details of what had occurred, but to no avail. Casca just said for him to wait until morning; then he'd know without being told.

That confused Sicarus, but he decided to wait until the morning to see what it was that Casca had meant about him finding out.

Returning to his hammock near Hrolvath, Casca lay down for a good night's sleep, content with the way things had turned out. It could have been much worse.

Casca was woken the next morning by a bellowing coming from Sicarus's direction on the upper deck. Grumbling, he hauled his butt up to the topside, where Sicarus was fuming. The glare of the new day hurt Casca's eyes. He squinted through them, trying to focus on the reddening face of Sicarus.

"What is it?" he mumbled through thick teeth.

Sicarus fumed at him. "Do you know what has happened since your return last night?"

Casca grumbled, "How the hell could I know anything? I've been asleep?"

Sicarus leaned closer to him, still shouting. "The praetor was found in his garden. His throat had been opened, and two of his personal slaves were standing over him, beating the body with branches. When the vigiles questioned them, they said everything was the fault of a scar-faced man who had attacked them and forced them to do the whipping. They claimed they never cut Cornelius's throat." Casca said nothing till Sicarus began to laugh. "I was told this by Cornelius's deputy, who said the slaves were obviously liars. He had them put to the sword before dawn for their crimes of murder and perversion."

Sicarus grinned evilly as he continued. "Oh, and by the way, the new commander asked me to extend his personal invitation for you to come to dinner any time you're in the neighborhood."

Casca joined Sicarus's grin with one of his own, replying smoothly, "Thank the deputy for me, but I think that you will probably have too many things for me to do around the ship for me to have any free time before we leave port.''

Sicarus agreed emphatically. ''You can bet your ass you're going to be busy. I think it is best we get loaded and get out of here as soon as possible.''

The new commander of Cyrene, Frontus, was a reasonable man who had for years loathed and detested the perversions of Cornelius Pompeianus. He and his sick harem had received the punishments they deserved. He wished the scar-faced man well, for he had done him a great service, and now he hoped to be confirmed in his new office as soon as word was sent to and returned from Constantinople.

With his cooperation, the loading of the requested supplies was sped up and the trireme and its escorts were able to take to sea that same night, to everyone's relief. The next stop would be Tripoli and a meeting with their commander in chief, the great Belisarius.

CHAPTER ELEVEN

Belisarius

At Tripoli, the ships were offloaded, to the relief of the men and the horses. Here they would stay long enough to give their animals time to regain their strength from the sea journey. Belisarius's army was spread out in a forest of tents. He had only twenty thousand regular soldiers to fight with, against what they estimated would be over a hundred thousand of the Vandals and their allies from the savage tribes of the desert.

Casca and Sicarus had grown closer during the short trip from Cyrene, and Hrolvath was seldom far away. He and Casca still spent most of their time fencing, but Casca knew that he would never be able to master the delicate techniques that a required a younger and more supple wrist to execute properly. He did find ways of countering Hrolvath's flickering sword point with less subtle moves of his own that made him nearly the equal of the young man, but not quite.

Sicarus chose Hrolvath and Casca for his escort, along with two of his other captains, when he was told to present himself to his general. They found Belisarius by searching for his standard that bore the eagles of the imperial house, set on the highest ground so that all who served him would be constantly re-minded that he was there watching over them and sharing their difficulties.

They were admitted into his tent by a guard from his personal troops. He greeted Sicarus with great affection, wrapping his arms about the mercenary's shoulders, hugging him as he would a long-lost friend. This gave Casca a chance to look over the last of the great leaders of the empire. At first glance, he was not very impressive, being of slight build and medium height with thinning brown hair, cut short. But the eyes were quick and full of lively intelligence and good humor. He had a smile that was infectious, and he welcomed Hrolvath and Casca easily. His movements were sure and certain, the mark of one who knows his mind and has little time for self-doubt. Casca could see why Sicarus had always spoken of him so highly.

The two leaders immediately went into a huddle after the introduction and greetings were finished. Sicarus asked first why he had chosen this time of year, when the rains were coming to the coasts, to make his attack. Belisarius informed him of his thought on the matter. With the rains due, many of the tribesmen would be busy at home with planting and care of their fields. Many of them would be reluctant to rally to the standards of the Vandals at this time. Casea and Hrolvath sat back, feeling privileged to be permitted to listen to the plans being discussed.

Most of the soldiers of Belisarius came from the provinces of Armenia, Isauria, Thrace, and Macedonia. Casca listened to the two men talk and learned of the changes that had taken place in the structure of the armies of the world since he had last fought with the forces of the empire. The heavy mounted trooper of the cataphracti was much the same as he had been in the past, whether in Persia or in Byzantium, wearing a steel cap mounted with a small crest and a long chain-mail shirt reaching from the throat to his midthighs. Gauntlets and steel shoes provided the balance of the armor. Over his mail there was usually a surcoat of light material. The soldiers in the front rank were also furnished with steel frontlets and poitrails to provide their horses with some protection in the assault. Their personal arms were a broadsword, a dagger, a short bow with a quiver of arrows, and a long heavy lance with ribbons of the colors on the bearer's surcoat and crest around the head to show which unit the bearer belonged to. The cataphracti, as all others, were organized into bands of four hundred fifty. Three bands made a turma.

The light cavalry was not as heavily equipped. Sometimes they had chain mail; other times they did not or wore only a light mesh cape that covered the neck and shoulders. Each one carried a large shield, which the heavy troopers did not, as they needed both hands to handle the heavy lance and guide a horse at the same time. The heavier armor had to take the place of a shield. The infantry was also organized into light and heavy categories. The heavy, known as the scutati, were protected by a steel helm and a short chain-mail shirt. The shield was a large oblong thing with the same colors on it as those of their turma or regiment. The principal weapon of the scutati was a heavy short battle-ax with a bladed front and spiked rear, with a dagger as a backup. They were covered by the light infantry, the psiloi, who were for the most part bowmen and able to use a larger and more powerful bow than the horse archers. This made them very effective against the enemy's horsemen. Some units, not very apt with the use of the bow, relied on javelins. For close work they carried an ax similar to the one of the scutati and a small round shield, or buckler, which hung from a strap at the waist.

The new armies of the Eastern Empire were small but very well organized. For every four cavalrymen there was a groom. For the infantry, every sixteen men were given an attendant who drove their cart, loaded with their supplies, rations, arms, and, if they were lucky on the way back, plunder. For each band, there were sixty picks and sixty shovels. Casca was relieved to see that the modern army had not lost its appreciation for the tactical values of the shovel.

This new force even carried with them litter bearers, known as scriboni, to take the wounded from the field. For this they received a nomisa—a small gold coin—for each man they brought in to the surgeons still alive. This novel innovation certainly helped the fighting man's morale. He was impressed with the new formations and the care that was being shown for the welfare of the warriors.

They learned that they would stay at Tripoli two weeks. Then, in a coordinated thrust, they would attack Carthage by both land and sea. Sicarus was to take his bands and land to the north of the city, to burn and pillage. By this action he would hope to draw off most of the city garrison to chase after them. Once the warriors of the Vandals were out of the city and far into the countryside, the mercenaries would make a large circle and return to join the main force under Belisarius, which would by then be in position to assault the walls. He had with him more than his usual complement of engineers, with their catapults and dart throwers; also, he had the secret weapon of the Byzantines, Greek fire, the composition of which was a most carefully guarded secret. With this, they would be able to throw fireballs over the walls of Carthage and set the city on fire, creating confusion and panic before the first of their men hit the walls with scaling ladders.

Once the mercenaries had returned, their primary task would be to harass the light cavalry of the Vandals, wearing them out until the heavily armored men and horses of the cataphracti could mass and ride them down.

Casca and Hrolvath were permitted to leave the two leaders alone to their planning and return to their ships to aid with the transferring of tents and supplies to the shore, where they were set up in an area separate from those of the regular army. Casca agreed that it was wiser to keep them apart, as there was normally little love lost between the higher-paid professionals of the mercenary bands and their contemporaries in the regular forces of the empire.

Once Sicarus returned to them, he called a meeting of his staff, many of whom had wondered exactly what position Casca would be placed in. Sicarus made him the senior instructor in swordplay and gave him some authority as his aide-de-camp. Casca had to take a couple of the mercenary captains out into the desert and whip their asses to establish his right to his new role. Luckily, they were reasonable men and only wanted to make certain that he was worthy of the honor shown him by Sicarus. Once that was established to everyone's satisfaction, there was no further trouble.

Although Hrolvath had no match in swordplay, Casca showed him the use of the pike and lance, teaching him how best to use his quick eyes and reflexes to the best advantage. The subject of his experiences at Cyrene was never discussed, but Hrolvath had taken on a new and stronger attachment to the scar-faced Roman.

During their stay at Tripoli, Casca had an opportunity to watch Belisarius at work. The man was everywhere, overseeing every detail of the forthcoming operation. He did everything he required of his men and usually did it better. Beneath his slight form was a deceptive strength of both body and will. Casca wasn't sure which was the stronger, not that it mattered. Belisarius was an exemplary leader of men and a fine tactician who believed in setting up rehearsals of proposed actions.

He had a wall built of sand, the height of a man's chest, to represent the walls of Carthage and its gates. For hours his ballistae and catapults were fired in order to learn the best angle to reach over the walls and fall on designated targets inside the city.

Casca understood the reasons for the man's successes in battle. He always planned ahead. Belisarius would not be caught unprepared by either good fortune or bad luck. Whichever the fates cast in his path, he would be ready for it.

He sat with Sicarus and Belisarius several times more before they again took ship. Both men and horses were reluctant to leave the security of the land for the wallowing, heaving ships, but they were given no choice in the matter. Bitching and complaining was as normal. They broke their tents to return with ill humor back into the bowels of the galleys and traders that would carry them to the north of Carthage for what they hoped would be their last sea voyage. Most would have preferred to have ridden or even walked the hundreds of leagues to and from their destinations rather than spend one more hour trying to keep their stomachs from crawling out of their mouths.

Once clear of Tripoli, the ships of their convoy swung far out to sea, avoiding the coast, where the single-masted warships of the Vandals prowled like sea wolves. When they were between Sicily and the African coast, they turned to the east and made a dead run, timed to reach the shore at the first hour of dark, when their movements would be less likely to be observed by watchers on the coast or ships at sea.

Anchoring in a small cove twenty miles to the north of Carthage, they remained on board until scouts returned to report that the beaches and cove were deserted. Then, once more, they had to offload their ships. This time there was no pier to make it easier. Equipment had to be rowed ashore in small lighters, and the horses had to be prodded with the points of swords to make them jump from the decks into the sea and swim for the beach.

It was finished in ten hours, and a secure base camp was laid out. Pickets and trenches were dug in the Roman fashion to provide security for the four hundred fifty men of the mercenary force. It would be the next day before the animals were settled enough to be of any real use. Before the camp was secured, the ships were already back out into the water, anxious to use the remaining hour of darkness to conceal themselves from the Vandal warships.

In the morning, new patrols mounted. This time they were sent out to scour the countryside. These, Sicarus had dressed in the costumes of the nomadic tribesmen of the region, hoping they wouldn't attract any attention or curiosity if they were seen. They had orders to avoid any contact with the populace. If they were approached, they were to run away, hoping that those who saw them would think them to be no more than Bedouins, who were not of an inclination to meet with strangers. That would not be an uncommon occurrence. Nomads were historically loners and not given to any more commerce with those outside their tribes than was absolutely necessary.

The riders began to return at varying intervals. Each had been sent out to different regions of varying distances. As they returned, they were questioned closely by Sicarus as to what they had seen. When the last of the scouts returned, he called together the captains of his bands to go over their plans.

Taking a map from a case, he pointed out their position and the location of known enemy garrisons and cities. From their place on the coast, they would be able to keep the forces of Hippo Regia tied up with the defense of their own city and prevent them from sending any reinforcements to the aid of Carthage when Belisarius moved on the city.

Belisarius had given Sicarus a free hand in the conduct of his harassing raids, with only general provisions that had to met in accordance with his timetable of operations.

Several of the captains wanted to split their forces to cover more terrain. This was vetoed by Sicarus, who flatly refused to split up his small force where they could be more easily cut up.

No, they would make a strong single raid toward Hippo Regia, burning and pillaging all the way. He wanted his men to spread out, giving the impression that there were thousands of them instead of the six hundred fifty of his reinforced bands. If they took civilians as prisoners, they were to let them go, but only after making certain they'd left the impression that thousands of warriors were on their way to attack Hippo Regia. By this ruse, he hoped the Vandals in Hippo Regia would keep to their walls, leaving them free to turn around and make a run for Carthage.

Before they pulled out, stockpiles of food and weapons were buried in the sands of the beaches. If they were successful and were able to make the ride back, they would have to replenish their stores.

Casca stayed close to Sicarus, and Hrolvath stayed close to Casca. They found little resistance as they moved across the fields of the African coast. Flames and smoke marked their passage as the fields were set to the torch. Noncombatants were not hurt physically if it could be avoided, but all were left thinking that a major force, numbering tens of thousands, was on the move, heading north. They drove the peasants before them, herding them to the walls of Hippo Regia. The Vandals believed the stories of the number of the Byzantine forces. Their own patrols had met with no success when they were sent out to reconnoiter. Most never came back, and those which did swore they had been outnumbered by at least twenty to one. The Vandals would not leave their city walls. Instead, they had sent by ship a cry for help to Carthage, asking them to send aid immediately, for they were in great danger of being overrun by the massive armies attacking them.

Once Sicarus was certain that his ruse was working, he turned his men around for the ride to the south. They had come within ten miles of Hippo Regia and now had nearly a hundred and thirty miles to cross before they would come in sight of Carthage. During their ride to the north, Casca had not once crossed swords with a Vandal. He did kill a couple of nomads who'd stumbled accidentally into the path of Sicarus. If they had just ridden on, they would have been left alone. But one had panicked and had tried to draw his bow for a shot at Sicarus. Casca was no more than forty feet from them and to their rear. He took both of them with easy casts from the javelins he carried in a quiver tied to the saddle of his horse.

The ride south was the exact opposite of the one to the north. They neither burned nor pillaged. This time it was a fast, orderly march. To join with the forces of Belisarius, they swung slightly to the east, taking them off the coast road so that they would not have to stop and engage enemy forces at every town and outpost.

Because of the roughness of the ground, it took four days for them to reach the first outriders of Belisarius's army. Sicarus reported to his leader immediately upon entering the camp. His men were left to their own devices under the watchful eyes of their captains till he returned with orders. Hrolvath and Casca walked to the beach to rinse the grime of the last days from themselves.

Belisarius greeted his friend once more, stating that he had arrived exactly on time, which was no more than what was to be expected when one dealt with Sicarus. Sicarus tried to apologize for his appearance, but his words were dismissed by Belisarius, who ordered drink and food to be brought. As he ate and drank, the other leaders of the army were sent for. Carthage was twenty miles away. From the top of the hills, the crenellated walls could be seen floating on drifting waves of desert heat.

The sides of the tent were raised to take advantage of the breeze from the sea. Chairs were set out as the leaders of his army made their entrance; the comes of the other two mercenary bands, Tortal of the Slavs, and Erlach of the eastern Goths, the regular officers of the heavy and light cavalry, and the infantry with their aides. Belisarius knew his men well, having personally selected each of them for this mission.

After making certain that his officers were all present and seated, Belisarius began his presentation, using a sand table with the features of the terrain they were to fight on reproduced in miniature atop it.

"Good afternoon, gentlemen." Using his baton of office as a pointer, he began to disclose his battle plans and repeated, to everyone's boredom, the reasons for their being where they were. "You all know that the city of Carthage has always been a thorn in the ass of the rest of world, no matter who sat behind her walls.

"It is not exactly the same as when Caesar ruled Rome, for we are not so dependent now on the grain of Africa for our survival. But as always, Carthage sits at the junction where her ships can control all passage to and from Spain, Gaul, and Brittannia. As you know, they are even now establishing their own colonies once more on the islands of Sicily and Sardinia. Once this is accomplished, they will have a stranglehold on the commerce and people of the western Mediterranean, effectively isolating us from those few cities which still pay Constantinople fealty. We will be completely isolated from the western reaches.

"It is bad enough that barbarians control the Italian mainland and most of Gaul and Spain, leaving us only our few small outposts as tokens. But those tokens are critical to us if we are to one day retake the Western Empire from the savages.

He nodded his head at two of his mercenary leaders, who were not from tribes noted for their table manners. "This naturally does not include any of our noble allies and friends."

The two tribesmen nodded their heads in understanding.

They didn't give a rat's ass whether the Romans thought them to be savages or not, as long as their gold was good.

Belisarius ran his baton up the coastline of Africa, from Egypt all the way to Pillars of Hercules, where the coasts of Africa and those of Spain were separated by only a short span of open water. "This," he said with determination, "could be our passage to the west once the power of the Vandals is broken. Gentlemen, we will secure that passage. Now let us see in what manner it can be done, and with the least loss of lives on our part."

CHAPTER TWELVE

Belisarius had his timing carefully arranged, but he still needed to draw the Vandals out of the city to avoid a protracted siege or the possibility of aid coming to them from their some-times friendly cousins, the Goths. He had sent out strong patrols to provide his force with a screen through which the Vandals, to his knowledge, had not been able to penetrate.

He had selected the site for his army with that in mind: a long cove with a rim of hills around it that gave him some protection from would-be observers. If he was successful in keeping the Vandal scouts from detecting his true numbers and disposition, perhaps there was a way to pull them out from the safety of their walls and into the open, where his better-disciplined forces could deal with them.

He gave the orders to advance to the walls of Carthage, but not with his entire force. He took only ten thousand of his men with him, leaving the cataphracti and mercenaries behind, along with much of the light infantry. Perhaps because of the messages from Hippo Regia, the Vandal king, Gelimer, chose not to meet them in the open. Gelimer had prepared as best he could in the short time he had since the first words of the Byzan-tine landings had come to him.

Sicarus and his bands were ordered to remain behind with the others till they were sent for. The engineers brought the siege machines within range of the walls under the cover of darkness. Belisarius wasted no time. As soon as they were in place, pots of Greek fire were hurled over the walls. Archers gave what support they could, not really wanting to do much damage. But it did give the impression that the city was under a determined attack.

The fires started by pots of Greek fire set many of the houses and buildings on fire, adding to the growing feeling of panic in Gelimer. It wasn't till dawn that he was able to see the forces of Belisarius laid out in an open field to the west. When he did, the sense of relief that there were so few Byzantines attacking him caused him to burst out in nearly hysterical laughter. If this was the grand army of Belisarius, he certainly would have no trouble dispatching them. He had those on the field below outnumbered by at least ten to one, and the arrogant fool hadn't even brought his best warriors with him. Without the cataphracti to deal with, his lighter, quicker warriors could ride circles around them, picking them off like doves. There would be no real threat to their center, which was usually the spot where the heavy cavalry used their weight to the best advantage, smashing through the enemy lines to the rear and creating a gap through which the rest of their forces could follow and roll up the flanks from the inside. Who did Belisarius think he was, Julius Caesar?

Still, Gelimer was cautious. He waited one day. Then two became three, and three turned into ten. No more warriors joined the forces of Belisarius, and he was convinced by his chieftains that Belisarius had his complete army at the walls.

Once he had determined what he believed to be the true strength of Belisarius's army, it was a different story. Calling his chieftains, he ordered his full army to prepare to attack through all the gates of the city. It would be easy to surround the belligerent fools below and then cut them down. Of one thing he was certain: Even if he fell, that pewling Christian Hilderic would not take the throne of the Vandals.

Belisarius kept in constant contact with those left behind by the usual system of having a series of mirrors set up to send signals. This was a most effective means of rapid communication, except when the days were cloudy. But that was not the norm in Africa. Here Belisarius could count on good days and fair skies.

It was with the flashing mirrors that the remaining host of his army was given the order to advance to an abandoned town called Ad Decimum, ten miles from Carthage. It was there that Belisarius had decided that the decisive battle would be fought.

Gelimer led his personal guard of warriors out the main gate as others exited through the other gates on either side of the city, joining to form a pincer in which he would crush the Byzantines like a walnut. It was with some surprise that he found an enemy that wouldn't fight. By taking only his light cavalry, Belisarius was able to conduct a fighting withdrawal, leading Gelimer farther away from his walled battlements. His siege machines he burned himself rather than let them fall into the hands of the Vandals. They were not the only ones he had in his arsenal, and they could be replaced by those still in the holds of his ships in the harbor.

Belisarius fought as a gnat does, nipping at the ears and face but never staying long enough to be swatted. He was always just out of reach. As he drew Gelimer to him, the bulk of his army moved into position at Ad Decimum. From the use of his sand displays, each unit knew its exact place to be, though they had never seen the area before. If Belisarius was correct, he should reach them within an hour, and right behind him would be the Vandal host in hot pursuit.

Near the town of Ad Decimum, on a broad plain with several large gullies to either side, the heavy infantry had been drawn up into a strong front line of three bands, with their men in ranks five deep with a gap of a hundred feet between them, to provide cover for Belisarius when he and his retreating forces reached them. Then they would deploy to either side to join the rest of the cavalry, which was set in hollows on either side of the flat ground, where they would not be seen by the pursuing Vandals. Sicarus and his men were on the right flank. Standing by their mounts on the right were the cataphracti, set so that they could attack the weak left of the Vandals. To the rear of the front line was also a reserve of two half bands behind the second rank of light infantry. The front line, if they saw that the first was giving way, was to wheel to the rear and form a support for the center as the reserve resisted any enemy attempts to turn their flanks.

A sound of drumming reached their ears. All ranks stood to arms, ignoring the growing heat of the day and palms that suddenly grew slippery with sweat. When the standard of Belisarius crested a low rise to their front, a cheer went up, but only from the center. Those in concealment had strict orders not to make any sound at all, on the pain of death. Belisarius and his force rode like the devil itself was after them once they'd seen the safety of their own ranks standing before them. The hooves of their animals raised clouds of dust that drifted over the plain, a gritty, eye-watering cloud. The light cavalry of Belisarius rode without hindrance through the gaps created for them, rushing straight to the rear, where they fanned out under the cover of their protecting forces to join their comrades on either flank.

Belisarius was in the forefront of the men to reach the security of their own ranks. He leaped from his tired horse to a fresh one and placed himself in the center of the second line. From there, he would be able to get a better idea of the manner in which the battle was progressing than he would if he was at the head of his cavalry in the middle of the fight. His courage was not in question. This was a time for brains to direct brawn.

With his cavalry placed in three separate units on both sides of the plain and out of sight, he would be able to maintain a great degree of flexibility in the manner in which he would conduct the battle. Although he was still outnumbered, the surprise element of having his main forces suddenly appear on the Vandals' flanks in large numbers once they had committed to an attack on his center—which he had no doubt they would—should give him the leverage he needed to make a complete sweep of the Vandal forces.

Gelimer halted his side-heaving charger on the same low rise from which the Byzantines had first seen Belisarius. He gave the signal for all to halt. His men drew up in a single linear mass, facing the Byzantines in front of them. He was surprised. There were more of the effeminate boy lovers out front than he had expected. Belisarius did have a reserve force. Gelimer scratched his beard, crushing a crippled flea in the process. He called his war chiefs to him. Between them, they made a count of the forces facing them and found that they still had an advantage of more than five to one; there was still no sign of the cataphracti.

For the most part, all he could see was some heavy infantry with archers backing them up. The horsemen in sight were those of Belisarius, who had been at the siege of Carthage. This, more than anything else, gave Gelimer the confidence to commit his warriors to a direct frontal assault. He still had a nagging feeling that he was being sucked in, even when he gave the order for his men to make their assault from out of their walls. Now he found that he had been right in his intuitions. Belisarius had been sandbagging him and did have a reserve; but that reserve was still not enough to resist the massed charge of his fifty thousand mounted Vandals. His own infantry was coming up behind them and would swell his force to nearly a hundred thousand.

Both sides gave themselves a needed breather before beginning the next round. Gelimer had to wait for his infantry, and Belisarius needed to give his horses a rest.

Aides were sent to all commands, telling them to wait for his trumpeters to give them their signals: a different call for each maneuver. Once the battle was engaged, the trumpets would be the only thing that would be audible over the sounds of battle.

They waited, each side gathering its strength and nerve. Mouths went dry and sticky, the gums tasting foul and greasy from the fear inside. Sweat ran in salty streams from spines and armpits.

Sicarus crawled on his belly, accompanied by Casca, to get a look at the Vandal line about four hundred yards away. At that distance, Casca could tell that they were not the same warriors he had faced in the forests of Germania or in the Balkans. Even from that distance, he could see that the heavy horned helmets were gone, as were the heavy hide shields. Now they wore mostly light, flowing robes in the manner of the Arabs and nomads.

From the Vandals, kettle drums began to beat, accompanied by the lighter thumps of the tambours of their native contingents. The Vandal infantry was approaching. It would be there soon. Horses stamped their hooves in anticipation; perhaps they, even more than the men, knew that soon the dry fields would be watered with blood.

It was difficult, but Belisarius had no choice; he had to wait for Gelimer to commit his forces to the attack before he could do anything. He moved among his men in the center, speaking to one and then another of the soldiers, giving encouragement to them, letting them know that he was with them and would be to the end. Whatever fate they encountered would also be his. If they won, he won. If they died, so would he.

Most of the infantry of Gelimer came from the tribesmen of the region who were either hired for service from their chiefs or had long memories for ancient wrongs done by Rome to their ancestors. They looked forward to the chance of spilling the blood of an old enemy. They were more like the Germanic warriors of the last century than the Vandals, being lightly armed with wicker or thatch shields. Few had any armor, and most relied on light throwing spears and long straight swords of poor steel or iron that often as not would bend when they struck against a proper shield. But they were still a force to be reckoned with, for their courage was great in the attack. They would not be broken or discouraged by the first failure or even the second.

But after that, if the Byzantine lines held them, they would lose their courage, for they believed that all failures and disasters came from the gods. If they couldn't win after two tries, the gods were against them and there was no sense trying again. That was why Belisarius had to hold. To be sure of victory, the center had to hold for two assaults before he could let loose his main force and his reserve. The natives, in loincloths and robes, marched on scaly hard soles across the field to join with the force of mounted Vandal cavalry. A trilling came from a strange manner they had of pursing their lips, making an eerie whistling noise in time with the beating of tambours and cymbals.

Belisarius knew that they would not wait long. The patience of savages is short. Once they arrived on the scene, he knew that Gelimer would have to advance soon, or his natives would begin to doubt him. Gelimer would lead the attack with his cavalry to punch a line in the Byzantine wall, creating an opening through which his infantry could swarm and break up the ranks of the Byzantines, dragging them down by sheer weight of numbers.

Gelimer, too, was familiar with the impatience of his native contingents. Once they arrived, he had to move. Placing them in a solid mass behind his horsemen, he began to advance slowly, giving them time to keep up with the riders, not wanting them too far behind when his cavalry hit the Byzantine center. The Bedouins picked up the beat of the hooves on their drums and added to it, gradually increasing the tempo, as if trying to force the cavalry on faster and faster. The tempo gradually ate its way into the minds and pulses of the riders and their horses. They increased their walk to a canter, loosening straps that held axes to their saddles or adjusting their grip on lances and javelins.

From a canter to a gallop, Gelimer was in the front rank, sword bared. There was no need for him to give orders; the heat of battle was beginning to set its own special time frame. Less than two hundred feet from the mainline of the Byzantines, the Vandals broke spontaneously and raggedly into a dead run, just in time to meet a hail of arrows from the second rank of the Byzantine line. Men and horse went down, some with over ten arrows sticking out of their bodies. The terrible screams of wounded and dying horses were easily heard over those of the men.

Belisarius was ready; this was it. The first rank of heavy infantry readied themselves, setting heavy spears to the earth, bracing for the assault of the horses. The second rank continued to send their shafts into the massed milling horde of Vandals.

The first rank was hit hard. The Vandal cavalry crushed in on them, trampling men under their horse's hooves. Then, driving on into the second rank, the Vandals ignored their own losses from the archers. They had only three more ranks to go, and they would be through the Byzantine line and able to come at them from their rear. The third rank was wavering, but still Belisarius held his hand. They would have to hold or all would be lost. The survivors of the third and second ranks fell back to the fourth. Vandals by the thousands threw themselves and their animals on it, but the massed heavy spear wall buried steel points into the chests of their horses, causing such congestion that it became hard for the Vandals to advance. The attack slowed. The archers of the rear increased their efforts, though some were beginning to fall to the lighter shafts of Vandal horse archers and those of the native infantry, which had bows.

The Bedouins surged around the front, trying to get inside, where their lighter arms would not be at such a disadvantage and they would be able to fight on more equal terms.

The flanks of the front line held. Giving a bit and then straightening out, the line moved back and forth like a thing alive. It thinned in spots and then filled itself again from those who pulled back. They held! The Vandals pulled back, leaving the wounded to be killed where they lay. The Bedouins wailed and cried for vengeance. Belisarius knew that they had to come again. This would be the one for the money.

Gelimer withdrew his force to a distance just out of the range of the Byzantine bowmen. He watched their lines carefully. They had almost broken through. He had lost many men, but he still had the numbers on his side. In the Byzantine lines, he could see weak spots now that were not being refilled. He believed that if Belisarius had any hidden resources, he would have had to use them by now. He didn't!

One more full-scale attack with all their strength, this time hitting the Byzantine front at three separate points, where he could see the line was weakest, should do it. He gave his men only a few minutes to let their horses breathe a bit easier, and then he gave the signal for the drums and cymbals to clash again. Once more they came on, screaming war cries from a land they had never seen. From their concealed position, Casca

heard the odd cry of Wotan and Odin come across the plains.
The Vandals, he saw as they neared, were still much the same in
the color of their hair, but their skins were darkened by their
years in the African sun till they could scarcely be told from the
dusky savage Bedouins at a distance. Their courage was still the
same, too, and they came on like the berserkers he had faced on
the Rhine.

Belisarius had his trumpeters standing by. He was wounded
slightly, from a javelin made with a reed haft and an iron head
that had grazed his cheek. Gelimer rose in his saddle, robes
flowing about him, the white of the robes blotched with blood
from those he had slain. He pointed his sword straight at the enemy and cried out for all to hear, "No quarter, no prisoners.
Kill them all!"

Sicarus signaled for his men to make ready, to mount and
ride. It would be soon. The others, on the far side of the plain
with the cataphracti, were doing the same. They knew what was
to be done, and if they failed this day, all would die or, even
worse, end up in the slave mines of the Vandals.

The scriboni were doing their jobs and clearing the Byzantine
wounded from the ranks, taking them to the rear. As they went
about their principal activity of saving the lives of their own
men, they also dispatched any Vandal or Bedouin who showed
the least sign of not being completely dead. This they did without charge, feeling that it was only right that they help where
they could. They were still in the front ranks when the next Vandal assault began. Several found that they couldn't get back
through their own reformed ranks, and so they picked up arms
that had fallen and placed themselves where they could do some
good.

The Vandals were totally committed this time. They knew
they could break through, and once they did, it would be all
over for the Byzantines. The first assault had done no more than
whet their appetites. Close behind, running low to the ground,
their native allies ran nearly as fast as the horses, not wanting to
miss out on any of the slaughter. They hit the first rank again,
this time massing their attack at the three spots Gelimer had indicated. The first rank went down, then the second and the
third. The fourth started to break, and some Vandals were actually through and heading to the rear when Belisarius finally
gave the order for his trumpeters to sound their signals.

At last, the cataphracti and mercenaries could get rid of their tension. They mounted and broke from their places of conceal-ment, swinging in behind the Vandal main force, trampling the native infantry underfoot. The surprise of their attack was all that Belisarius had planned for. The Bedouins gave up, wailing like lost souls, and ran back the way they had come, leaving the Vandals alone and isolated on the battlefield.

The cataphracti hit the left side of the Vandal column, break-ing it into several pieces, and then wheeled and turned in a mass, smashing those nearest the main line of the Byzantine in-fantry. At this point, Belisarius released his reserve to fill the gaps the Vandals had made in his lines. Once more he had a sol-id front. His mobile forces were herding the surprised Vandals into small groups that could be easily taken care of by archers, and his ax men provided the anvil against which the cavalry played the hammer.

Sicarus and his men swung far out to the rear of the Vandals, blocking their way back to the safety of the walls of Carthage. Casca stayed close to Sicarus, thinking that his job was more to make sure that he didn't get killed than to take out a Vandal or Bedouin. Hrolvath had the same idea. The three of them led their own attack at the head of their bands, cutting off nearly a hundred Vandals and herding them back into the fray, where the archers could dispose of them with little loss to their own men.

Hrolvath and Sicarus gained some added respect for Casca when they saw him grab a Vandal by the neck, lift him off his horse, and snap the warrior's spine over his saddle while still riding. Casca's good strong arm kept death away from Sicarus more than once that day, and Hrolvath's long toothpick danced and pinked, taking out an eye here, leaving a tiny hole in a sav-age throat there.

The mercenaries did their job well that day, as did the rest of the army, but there was no way they could contain all the Van-dals when they'd finally broken completely and had run for it. Nearly five thousand made it back to Carthage. First among them was Gelimer, who as soon as he returned made his first act that of killing Hilderic by slitting his throat and then tossing the body over the battlements.

Belisarius sent runners to tell Sicarus and the others to ease their attacks on the Bedouins and allow some of them to reach Carthage. If he knew them at all, they would be more trouble than they were worth once they were inside the walls. They were not worth a damn when fighting from fixed positions.

They felt trapped and became demoralized easily when they didn't have open ground around them.

Sicarus told his captains to finish off any stragglers they came across. He personally was going to go to Belisarius to see whether there was anything more for them to do. As they rode, Casca could see isolated bands of beaten warriors on horseback and foot, heading away from the battlefield of Ad Decimum in any direction that was open to them.

They came around a clump of brushlike trees, twice the height of a man, and were jumped by a half dozen Bedouins, who most likely only wanted their horses so that they could make better time getting away from the mop-up squads scouring the brush. Sicarus split one's head to the neck with a well-placed blow of his broadsword and then was pulled from his horse by a wild-eyed, wooly-haired, naked thing who swarmed over him like a gangly brown spider, screaming and frothing at the mouth. Hrolvath stabbed him seven or eight times through the back before he finally let loose. Casca kept the others at bay, with his horse whirling around them, screaming like a demon of the desert, his heavier sword crushing arms and clavicles as his charger pawed the air, doing its part with steel-shod hooves. The surviving natives changed their minds about the horses and took off on foot, only to be brought down by a flock of arrows from a half band of light archers who were in pursuit of the Vandals but not so picky that they would pass up the easy targets presented by the backs of the fleeing Bedouins.

By the time they reached Belisarius, it was all over, save for the last of the Vandals, who were so critically wounded that they couldn't be saved. Belisarius did stop the slaughter long enough to take five thousand prisoners. He had plans for them later. Most of them would be sent to Constantinople and forced into a light cavalry unit to fight on the distant borders of Byzantium, against either the Persians or the tribes of Carpathia.

Once they had cleaned up the field, he sent his full army back to Carthage, where once more they camped in sight of the crenellated battlements. This time Belisarius knew that he would be able to get over them. The losses at Ad Decimum were so large that the enemy couldn't keep him from getting his men over the top. They would not have enough experienced warriors left to guard the six and half miles of wall with any degree of strength. Now it was just a matter of a few days before it would all be over and he would have his victory completed. The news that Hilderic had been killed didn't upset or surprise him. He knew that Hilderic had just been an excuse to wage war against the Vandals; the real reason had been the one he had told his captains before the fight.

For Casca it had been an easy fight, and he was glad he hadn't had to take too great a part in it. He would enjoy the respite before the final assault on the walls of Carthage. It gave him time to think about Ireina and Demos. He wondered how they were getting on at the farm. He knew that Demos would have a good time with the young animals there, playing with goats and wrestling baby pigs in the mud. He would be glad when this was over and he received his share of the booty. The coffers of Carthage should give him what he needed to buy them their farm.

With luck, this was the last time he would have to leave them, at least until he began to see the questions in their eyes about his not aging. He knew that Ireina would not really think anything about it, as she already thought of him as some sort of godling, but he didn't want Demos to know him as anything other than a father who one day went off to war somewhere and didn't return. That would be the easiest answer for the youngster to deal with and understand and the best solution he could think of, though it still hurt to think that one day he would lose them.

CHAPTER THIRTEEN

Timoteus, secretary to the magister officorum, caught his breath as he read the intercepted letter from Belisarius to the emperor. Holding not only the title of the master of offices but also that of the cursus (imperial post), Gregory was able to monitor at will any correspondence to and from the palace that he wished to, and the missives of Belisarius and his army were of great interest. He was not pleased with the growing popularity of Belisarius. It took away from the influence of the eunuch faction of the palace and cast their own achievements into a lesser light in the eyes of the emperor.

Timoteus bit his lower lip in consternation. Should he wake his master for this? The contents of the letter, reporting on the Vandal campaign, were innocuous enough. It simply stated that victory was theirs and that he, Belisarius, wished to call the attention of his emperor to the valiant service rendered the empire by those who had fought under his standard. Among the names were those of the mercenary chieftain Sicarus and the one that gave Timoteus such a problem, especially with the threat of major disaster hanging over the city. Plague had once again reared its head, though it was for now found only in the poorer quarters of the city. Perhaps it would go away, as it sometimes did, to reappear in later years, even more deadly. It was not unusual for there to always be a few cases of it around, but this looked as if it could be a major breakout of the death. He truly didn't know which the master would think the more important: the potential deaths of tens of thousands or the name he was looking at.

Casca! Could it be the one the master had searched for these many years? He had doubted in his heart whether the mythical killer of Jesus really lived, even when reports of one resembling him came to them from their agents. But now the name

127

screamed at him. *Casca!* With some trepidation, he knew that he would have to disturb the slumber of Gregory.

Taking the letter from Belisarius with him, he left his chambers to walk to the next apartment, which was the master's, who liked to have his secretary close to him in the event that his services were required at any hour of the day or night. Holding his breath, he rapped on the door, his actions watched by a eunuch warrior.

His mild tapping was immediately responded to by a terse, "Enter." He sighed, relieved that the master was still awake. Entering, he bowed his head as he approached Gregory, who was sitting behind his desk going over his most recent correspondence with Narses, his eunuch general from Persarmenia, holding the office of the sacellarius and, as such, the commander of the Sparthos-cublicars. Known only to a few was the fact that Narses was a member of the Inner Circle and had been brought to his position of power by the careful, patient machinations of Gregory. In his capacity as sacellarius, he was in position to remove the emperor by force at any time it suited their purposes.

"What is it, my son, that keeps you up this late hour?" Gregory's voice always had the same flat fatherly tones, except when he was in a rage.

Timoteus indicated the name of Casca on the letter, saying nothing. Gregory's face paled and then flushed. Sweat broke free from his pores to glisten on his forehead.

"When did this come in?" He rose from his desk to confront his secretary."

"Not ten minutes ago, master," came Timoteus's tremulous response. "It was in a packet of correspondence from Carthage brought to the palace this night."

Gregory crumpled the document in his hands, holding it to his chest as he raised his eyes to the vaulted ceilings of his chambers. "Praise be to Jesus and his disciple Izram. The beast has been found."

Clearing his throat, Timoteus dared to interrupt the ecstasy of his master. "There is one other thing in the message, lord. It has to do with the wife and child of the man Casca."

Gregory whipped his head around, his eyes wide, locking on those of his secretary. "Wife? Child?" His tones changed from exultation to the hiss of a viper.

Straightening out the document, he read through it carefully till he came to the part mentioned by Timoteus. The letter asked for the emperor to show his loyal servants the great favor of forwarding the information that they were all right to the wife of Sicarus and that of his good servant Casca Longinus, whose wife and son were staying at his home in the country.

Gregory called for slaves to light the rest of the lamps in his rooms. There would be no sleep this night. He had much to think of. Timoteus was dismissed to return to his quarters, with the orders to stand ready for new instructions. All that night, Gregory went over in his mind all that he knew of the beast. Never in any of the writings passed down had there ever been any mention of the killer of Jesus siring a child. Did that mean that he couldn't? Perhaps his information was not complete. The implications of the possibility that Casca could have children was staggering. If the beast had one child, he could have more, and if he did, would they too carry the curse that Jesus had put upon their sire? If they did, and they passed their inheritance on to their offspring, they would multiply by the tens of thousands, till they had control over the earth, and none would be pure of their contamination.

He would have to find out. His mind was made up; there was only one thing to do. The woman of Casca and the child would have to be brought to him for testing. Bursting out of his doors, he startled the guard as he went to Timoteus's room and shoved the door open, scaring his already edgy secretary. He shouted for him to get his ass dressed and ready to travel; he had a message to deliver to Narses this night.

Timoteus hustled to obey. By the time he was ready, Gregory had a letter for him to deliver to the hand of Narses and no other. At the barracks of the Sparthos-cublicar, he acquired two warriors for escorts and took horse for the encampment of Narses and his command at the Valley of Olives, where his castrati were practicing mounted maneuvers and close-order drill as part of their annual training exercises.

It was the second hour past dawn when he reached the picket lines of the Sparthos-cublicar and, after identifying himself and his escort, was admitted to the camp.

Narses had been about his duties long before dawn. He prided himself on being the first of his officers to rise. It paid well, for that was the time when men and minds were the slackest; if mistakes were to be made, most of them would occur at those times. It also kept his sentries in a constant state of alertness, for if he found them asleep at their posts, they would never wake from their slumber. After the death of three sentries in two years, there had never been another recurrence of such a dereliction of duty in his command.

Narses was small in stature; his uniforms and armor were always of the best quality. The thinness of his features gave lie to the myth that all eunuchs were fat and lazy. There was nothing fat or lazy about him or any in his command. They had beaten fierce enemies, among them the tribesmen of the Gepids, Lombards, and Huns. His face was that of an aristocrat, cold, haughty, supremely confident in the abilities of his mind and personality to overcome all difficulties.

All his life had been prepared for one thing only: to be of service to the Brotherhood of the Lamb. He had not hesitated a heartbeat before giving permission for the knife to remove his testicles. What were the few feeble pleasures that a slut could give him in comparison with the great mission that awaited him as a disciple of Izram? His name be blessed!

He recognized the secretary of Gregory immediately and had the man fed as he read the missive from the Elder. It gave him no reason for what he was to have done, but the urgency was clear. It must be of extreme importance to the order. It would be done.

Summoning two of his most trusted captains, he gave them their orders. They would take with them two full squads of the Sparthos-cublicar, and those must all be Brothers of the Lamb.

The captains, Aeolius and Miklos, had no questions about why they were to ride to the farm of Sicarus and take the woman and boy child there to the magister, nor did they question the order that all else there must be put to the sword and for it to look like a bandit raid was responsible for the slaughter.

By the time Timoteus had returned to the capital, the warriors of Narses were already outside the fields of the farm of Sicarus. They halted their horses to discuss their strategy before going in. Once the two captains had agreed on a method of accomplishing their mission, they formed their troops into two columns and led them through the gates with no signs of anxiety or urgency. After all, they wore the uniforms and armor of the Sparthos-cublicar, whose members were often entrusted as bodyguards to the emperor and his family.

Once inside, they were greeted by the wife of Sicarus, who accepted at face value their story that they were on the trail of traitors who had been seen in the area. She agreed to call in all her field workers and house servants. When asked if there was anyone else on the premises, she admitted to having a guest and her child staying with her, saying with pride that her guest's husband was serving her own man at the siege of Carthage.

The officers of the Sparthos-cublicar were very polite but insistent that their orders required that they ask everyone they met about the traitors and whether they had been seen. Even the child might have seen something he had not told his elders, thinking it of no importance. She sent for Ireina and Demos. There was no reason for her not to honor their request. Even if they were eunuchs, they did have beautiful manners.

The field workers and house staff were assembled in the patio as Ireina and Demos came out of the house. Aeolius, the elder of the two captains, inquired if she was the wife of the man known as Casca and if the boy with her was his son. Once she had acknowledged this, he whispered in her ear that he had a message for her from Casca and that it was for her ears only. To avoid any interference from the wife of Sicarus or any others, they had worked out a plan. Using the guise of searching for traitors, they would question each member of the farm individually. To this end, all had been lined up single file to wait their turn.

The first was the wife of Sicarus. Unsuspecting, she obeyed the request for her to go inside the house to the inner storeroom, where she was quickly and silently stabbed to death by the castrati of the Sparthos-cublicar. One at a time they repeated this process till all were put to the sword. Ireina knew nothing of this, as she and Demos were quickly put on horseback and taken away from the farm before they could have any hint that murder was being done to those who had sheltered them. Her questions as to what the message from her husband was about were silenced by gags in the mouths of both her and her son. As they crested a small hill, she looked back to the farm, from which tendrils of smoke were already rising as the buildings were put to the torch and the dead were scattered about the grounds to add credence to the story that bandits had raided the farm.

Ireina and Demos were brought to the home of Gregory and there were placed in rooms that were guarded by carefully selected members of the Brotherhood. Gregory spent many hours watching them through hidden eye slits, trying to see whether there was anything about them that was different from other humans. The child especially drew his attention. He wondered time and again if the young boy carried the seeds of immortality in his blood.

He rejoiced in his soul that he had the means to bring the spawn of Satan to him. He had locks of their hair, both mother and child, brought to him to be included in the message that he would send to Carthage.

For that mission, he selected the captain of the Sparthoscublicar who had destroyed the farm of Sicarus. This was an added precaution in the event that Casca didn't believe the letter or the hair. The captain would be able to give him their descriptions in such detail that there could be no doubt as to the truth of the letter.

Casca would come to him, and soon. Gregory delayed as long as he could the testing of the child but at last gave in to his desire to know the truth. Once the letter was sent, there was no longer any need to delay. He had to find out.

Ireina was dragged before Gregory, who sat on a plain curule-shaped chair of dark wood, his soft features looking like those of a parent who has to lecture an unruly child.

Shaking off the hands of the guards, she faced the man who had ordered her taken from Sicarus's wife and brought here with their son. It was a relief finally to be able to face the one responsible. The not knowing was worse than anything she could imagine. At last, she hoped to find the reason for her captivity.

Gregory knew what was in her mind and answered her questions before she had a chance to speak them. He pursed his fingers under his round chin and spoke to her gently.

"Child," he began, "you have brought to us that which Casca will come after: you and your child."

Ireina broke in spontaneously, "Our child?"

Gregory halted his prepared statement. His eyes narrowed into puffy slits as his voice lowered to even more gentle and softer tones, yet the venom behind the easy words was unmistakable. "Our child? Yours and Casca's?"

Ireina didn't know why, but she was suddenly more afraid than she had ever been; yet she would not deny her own son and his father. Straightening her back, she responded with passion, "Yes, ours. Mine and Casca's! What is that to you?"

Gregory pulled his hood over his head to conceal his face. This was something that would require thought. If what the woman said was true, they were faced with a problem even more pressing than having Casca come to Constantinople.

He ignored Ireina's protestations and waved her out of his presence. Her cries were muffled by a calloused hand as she was dragged back to her cell in the cisterns.

Gregory made his excuses to the palace, claiming illness. He prayed for four days and nights on his knees on the stone floor. He had set out the spear of Longinus to aid in him in his devotions. Neither food nor wine did he take. He fed on the passion of his soul, trying to reach out to the spirit of God and find what he must do.

His fevered brain tossed, turning in on its own fantasies and fears. He heard a thousand voices speaking to him from all around, within and without his being. He prayed for guidance, and it came. There was one answer to his problem, and it could be settled by a simple test.

If the brat was the child of the godless one, had he inherited the curse with his blood? Could the spawn of Satan sire a whole race of immortals that would one day do battle against the righteous armies of Jesus on the day of the resurrection?

If there was the remotest possibility of that, he had to stop it. He must find out, and the answer was simplicity itself, as the truth always is.

Rising from his devotions, he went to his couch and slept the good sleep of the devout servant who serves his master well. When he woke, all would be made clear.

With the dawn he rose and performed his ablutions, dressing carefully in his finest robe of white linen, his scrubbed face cherubic and friendly. After he had breakfasted, he called for the boy to be brought to him in his study.

Young Demos was brought to him, still rubbing the sleep from his six-year-old eyes, wondering why he had been taken from his mother and why they were here. No one had hurt them, but he didn't understand why they kept him from going out to play or why his mother held him so close in her sleep and cried so hard when the tall men came for him and took him away.

He was shown into the study by Gregory's personal secretary, a tall blond man with bland features that betrayed no emotions, only blind obedience to the laws of the Brotherhood.

Gregory gave Timoteus permission to leave and then smiled gently at the child and motioned for him to come closer to his table. The child was handsome and had a body that would grow square and strong. His eyes were a darker blue than his mother's, and his hair likewise was brown instead of her silver.

Gregory spoke pleasantly to the boy, who showed no fear at being alone with him. The Elder gave him fresh fruit and sweet-meats to eat as he examined the child from every angle, looking for any sign that this was indeed the child of evil.

Gregory could see only that he bore more of a resemblance to someone else than he did to his mother, and the woman swore that he was the child of Casca. Gregory sat back on his chair and sighed. There was only one way to be absolutely certain.

Calling the boy to him, he said easily, "Come here, child, and sit with me. I'll tell you a story."

Demos did as he was bade and climbed into the lap of the smiling, friendly man who offered to peel him an orange and tell him a story. Gregory stroked the soft, brown, curling hair of the child and touched the fair unscarred skin with easy fingers. He held the child gently to him and told him a story of a warrior who had sinned greatly against God and had passed this way many years before and had gone on to reach the wall that runs forever and beyond that to the lands of China and how he had returned but, when he did, brought back with him a great evil.

Demos lifted his eyes from his half-eaten orange to ask, "What evil was that, sir?"

Gregory held the child close to his chest with his left arm and whispered into the child's ear, "You!"

Swiftly, he slid the knife, concealed in the cushion of his chair, straight into the innocent heart of the trusting child, sinking the blade into its hilt. He held Demos to him in a firm grip as the boy quivered gently and died, his mouth opening to let fall a piece of bloody orange onto the clean white robes of the Elder.

Gregory lay the small body down on a couch and moved his chair to sit by him. Now it was time to wait. He removed the tunic from the child's chest that he might see the wound. If the wound healed, the child was Casca's. If the boy didn't return to life, he had saved an innocent child from a life of being corrupted by the spawn of evil that was Longinus. This way, the child was a martyr and would sit at the foot of God in heaven.

All that day and through the night, his eyes never left the pale body of the child, and the wound stayed open. There was no sign of healing or a return of the life force. By the dawn, Gregory was convinced that the child was truly dead. He said a mass for his spirit and called for the body to be removed and disposed of. The servant who had brought Demos in came and wrapped the tiny remains in a small rug and took him away. The waters of the Bosphorus would conceal their act for all time.

Now Gregory wondered about the woman. Perhaps he should dispose of her too. No! She might make Casca more tractable as a hostage, and then he would be more likely to be obedient to their wishes.

The woman would live a while longer. He would tell her that the child had been sent away to live on a farm until Casca came to claim them. Then they would be reunited. There was no sense having a hysterical mother on his hands. He knew that to give Ireina even the tiniest of hopes would make her easier to control.

A cry vibrated over the desert surrounding the broken walls of Carthage. Holding the locks of hair from Ireina and Demos in his hand, Casca felt his entire body shaking in white rage. Aeolius believed that all that was keeping him alive was the fact that the child and its mother were being held hostage by the Elder.

In that supposition, Aeolius was mortally wrong. If the Elder wanted him, Casca knew that the messenger was of no importance once he had delivered his message. But he was of great importance to Casca. He advanced on Aeolius, eyes narrowed to piggish slits, face pale as he removed the thin, slightly curved skinning knife from its scabbard.

Aeolius started to move away. The madness in Casca's eyes made him doubt the length of his remaining time on earth. A blow from a knotted fist struck the thin bone behind his ear, paralyzing him. He was awake but couldn't force his limbs to obey the commands he kept giving them to run or crawl. Strips of cloth wrapped about his wrists and feet ensured that he would remain immobile. Before he could regain control of his vocal chords, a rag was stuffed in his mouth.

Casca leaned over him, whispering, ''You're going to tell me everything, and then I'll let you die. But not too soon. First, you're going to suffer, to know pain such as you have never dreamed of. Then and only then will I give the mercy of death.''

The skinning knife went to work. In his centuries, Casca had taken the hides from hundreds of animals. This was his first and only human. He took his time making the slits under the skin, drawing the blade delicately along the strip running from the neck to the tip of the shoulders. Then, easing the thin blade under the skin till he could get a grip on it, he began the slow, care-

ful process of pulling and then slicing a bit more to loosen the
flesh from the outer hide.

Aeolius was ready to talk before the first square inch of skin
had been sliced from his body, but he couldn't speak. The gag
in his mouth became clotted with his own blood where he
chewed at the sides of his mouth in agony. Casca had seen this
process in several places. He knew how to take his time and
when to stop to give the subject a bit of a rest before continuing.

By this time he had peeled the skin from the back of the captain to where it now hung, a red wet flap around the man's
waist, leaving his upper torso a mass of red and blue veins,
nerve endings that screamed at the slightest touch, even at
Casca's hot breath as he worked with single-minded mania.

Aeolius was near the edge of madness himself. Seeing this,
Casca knew that it was time to stop. The captain would answer
all his questions. He forced back the hate from his mind to gain
enough control to ask the questions he needed to have answered. Aeolius did as Casca had foretold. He spoke of everything: of the Sparthos-cublicar and their raid on the farm of
Sicarus, of the slaughter done there, and of how the woman of
Casca and her child had been taken to Constantinople to the Elder, who was also the magister officorum. He spoke till Casca
lived up to his bargain and gave him an end to pain by taking his
thin blade and severing the nerves between the vertebrae at the
rear of the captain's neck.

It was in this state that Hrolvath found him; he nearly threw
up after getting a good look at the bloody thing lying on the floor
of Casca's tent. Casca had to forcibly sit Hrolvath down and explain what had taken place. He told him only that he had enemies from many years back and that they had taken his wife and
son hostage and would kill them. What he had done was necessary to find out where they were being held.

Hrolvath still avoided looking at the raw draining thing that
had been a man. But it was a violent world they lived in, and if
that was what had to be done, he had enough faith in his friend
to try to understand it. The clincher came when Casca told him
that Sicarus's farm had been destroyed and all there, including
his wife, put to the sword by the same men who had taken Ireina
and Demos.

Hrolvath promised to keep what had happened secret. He
helped Casca haul the body out to the battlefield to let it lie with
those of the Vandals, where there was little likelihood that any-

one would take notice of one more among the thousands.

Hrolvath gave Casca what money he had and escorted him to the docks to buy passage on the next ship for Constantinople. Hrolvath didn't know whether he should have told Sicarus of the loss of his wife.

Casca made up his mind for him, saying flatly, "There is nothing he can do for his wife or servants now, but Belisarius still needs him here. He will find out soon enough. When he does, then you can tell him that I have gone to take revenge on those who did it for both of us."

He left a bewildered and stunned young man behind as he went to find a ship to take him back to Constantinople. Carthage no longer held any interest for him. That would remain for Belisarius to clean up. He had something to do in the city of Justinian that could not wait one second longer for anyone or anything. He could be in Constantinople in a week.

CHAPTER FOURTEEN

Casca spoke to no one when he had to change ships at Chrysopolis, on the Asian side of the Bosphorus, for the short ride across the straits to Constantinople. Paying his fare, he found a place on the bow where he could see the far shore. In the distance, rising over the sky, he could see dark tendrils of oily smoke rising to the sky. The capital was dying. Plague walked the streets of Constantinople. Plague, the most democratic of killers, sparing neither child nor warrior, noble or slave; the messenger of death touched every door.

The thought of Ireina and his son inside those walls made him sick to his stomach. He had seen the handiwork of the disease many times. Those who had done this thing would pay. Of that he was certain. In his mind, anger burned red, setting his teeth grinding against each other, the muscles in his jaws working constantly. His hand touched his sword, gripping the hilt so hard that he nearly bent it. Someone was going to pay, and if they had hurt Ireina and his son, there would not be enough blood in their bodies to settle the score.

The sails of the shallow-draft vessel flapped listlessly. Slaves had to help it along, their oars slapping in series against the darkening waters, each stroke of the sweeps sending him closer.

He didn't see the small dark shape in its sack that had recently come back to the surface of the waters as if waiting to greet someone as it rode gently in the hollow of a wave that lightly bumped the ferry. Then it was gone, taken back into the deep. As they neared the bank, the wind shifted slightly. He smelled the taste of death, the sweet, cloying odor of decay and smoke. He saw lines of wagons and hand-pushed carts on the road carrying their cargoes of bodies to be dumped into the waters of the Bosphorus.

The ferry pulled up to the wharf on the Thracian side, and Casca was over the bow and on the dock before the boat stopped moving. Sandaled feet slapping the wet stones, he rushed past the porters and slaves waiting to offload the ferry. He ignored the gruesome carts and their cargoes. There was nothing he could do for them, but there might still be something he could do for his own. The Brotherhood wanted him to come to them; by all the demons of hell, he was here. They would live only long enough to wish that they had left him alone. He reached the walls just minutes before the gates would have been shut. Soldiers of the palace garrison lined the access to the gates, making certain that all slaves who had left the city returned. By order of Justinian, no one was to be permitted to leave until the death had run its course. No one, that is, except the rich and powerful, who were retreating to their villas and estates.

As Casca passed through the gates, one of the guards fell face forward on the stones. An order was shouted out by a corporal, and the man's body was hefted by slaves onto a cart to lie with those of a family of Byzantine merchants. Only his weapons were removed from him and handed over to the corporal.

Beating and cursing his way past the weary, foot-dragging slaves, he passed under the eye of the portal guards, who didn't ask to see his papers. They had only been ordered to stop anyone from leaving, not entering, though why anyone would come to this place now, they didn't know and didn't care. Most of them had escape on their minds, and the rate of desertion among their ranks was rising every day. Only the promise of more gold kept any of them at their posts.

Plague! The mere mention of the word could turn even the bravest of men into puling cowards. Casca had seen it more than once. On the side of the streets he saw the bodies of dead rats lying about. When the rats began to die, humans were next. He didn't know why, but always in the past it was known that the rats began to die first; then came the sickness to people, as if in their death the rats passed on whatever it was that killed.

Yellow clouds of sulphur smoke drifted through the streets, where only the death slaves worked, hauling bodies out of buildings and alleys to load them on carts. Down the Via Honorius, he could hear the ringing of a hand bell as a shrill voice cried out to the buildings on either side, "Bring out your dead, bring out your dead."

Casca stepped around a pile of bodies. One of them, a woman

in her thirties, was still wearing a bracelet of gold set with large stones of amber. Many of the slaves would acquire enough wealth from the looting of bodies to buy their freedom, if they survived. He covered his nose and mouth with the edge of his cloak to keep out the terrible stench of bodies that had lain too long before being found. The heavy sweetness of decay was impossible to avoid.

Added to the thin pealings of the deathmonger's bell came the heavier, more vibrant tone of the bells of the cathedrals of Constantinople, where masses were being held day and night. He knew that the churches would be crowded with the sick and the well—the one praying to be healed, the other not to get sick—and in their hearts each of them hoping that if someone had to die, let it be the one next to him, that he himself might be spared. He also knew that the death passed most quickly where people were close together in crowds or groups. Turning a corner, he knocked over the body of a priest who had died sitting up, still in his brown cassock, hands folded together in the act of prayer. The face was thin and yellow. His tongue, black and swollen, protruded between the teeth.

The dark was gathering quickly, throwing into shadows the narrow corridors of the streets. Casca knew that the palace of the magister would be well guarded, but he thought he knew how to get by. Gregory expected him to come knocking politely on his door and beg permission to enter. Casca would not accept that invitation, even though they held Ireina and his son. He knew that the word and honor of the priests of the Brotherhood was good only as long as it served their purposes; they were not to be trusted. He would see Gregory, but on his own terms.

From the houses on either side he would occasionally hear the sounds of mourning as someone grieved over a dead parent, lover, or child. Several times he saw doors furtively open for a moment as a body was hauled out to be added to the hundreds that still lay uncollected. Then there was the sound of the doors being shut and bolted.

Pulling his cloak over his head to conceal his features, Casca tried to get his thoughts organized. It was hard to avoid the temptation to just barge in and take his family back from them. But good sense dictated that he wait a while longer, until the early hours before the next dawn, when eyes were the heaviest among guards who would be half asleep waiting for their relief to come. He took the street leading to the palace of Gregory in order to take a look at the layout before finding somewhere to hole up till it was time for his visit. The streets were emptying of what few had dared to leave their homes. In the distance he could smell smoke from a fire that consumed a series of apartments. The fire would last until it burned itself out. There would be no one this night to put the flames out.

On the high ground, where the officials and favorites of the court kept their palaces, the signs of death were less obvious. The streets were clear of bodies, but the aura of the plague was not to be denied; it had visited here, too. He stayed to the shadows, not wishing to give any watchful eyes warning that he had arrived. They would find out soon enough. The palace of Gregory was not the largest there, but it had high walls on which he could see dim figures, which meant that there were guards who still served their master.

He made two passes, each an hour apart, circling the palace. There were two entrances, neither of which he could use. He would have to go over the wall. There were no trees to climb or anything near enough to them that he could climb to and then jump from. He would have to think of another way to scale the walls. In spite of his anger, which had now settled down into a deep dull pain, he knew he would need to rest before finishing his business. Leaving by the Via Augustinus, he went back to the main city to find a hole for the next few hours.

A two-story villa from which he could see no lights showing had its front door open, swinging on loose brass hinges and inviting him inside. He kicked away two pariah dogs that were worrying at the body of an old man near the steps. Removing his sword from its scabbard, he entered the dark atrium, closing the door behind him and latching it. Stopping, he held his breath to hear better, turning his head first one way and then the other to see if he could catch any sound that might mean others were in the house with him. He was tired, but instinct and habit made him search the house from room to room. In the kitchen, he found the desiccated body of a woman lying by the fireplace used for cooking. Her clothes were rich, of fine carded wool with silk threads woven into the cloth. In the bedroom he found the body of a man and woman lying together side by side. He was glad it was dark so that he didn't have to look at them. The odor was enough to make a vulture ill.

In the last room, at the rear of the second floor, he found one other corpse, that of a younger man, judging from the build, lying near a chest of carved dark wood. Obviously, the dead man had been trying to get to the chest. Therefore, it had to be important. Casca moved the body out of the way by pulling the man's sleeve. Once the body was clear, he opened the chest after breaking the lock with a twist of his sword blade. The chest contained articles of jewelry, silks, and several small bags of silver and gold.

The man had been trying to get to it when the death took him. Perhaps it would serve another purpose. Casca removed the chest, carrying it with him to an empty room, where he made a thin pallet of his cloak and lay down to get what sleep he could until it was time to go. He had his plan worked out for getting over the wall without being spotted before he went to sleep. He set his mental clock for the right number of hours to rest before awakening.

At the right moment, his eyes clicked open; he was instantly alert. It was the right time. He had two hours before dawn. Scrounging around the room, he found a lamp made of terra cotta. Striking off the flint from his fire kit onto a patch of lint, he ignited the oil in the lamp. By the thin red glow, he was able to go through the chest and remove the items he would need later. The silver and gold he put into his own, nearly empty pouch, keeping one sack of each to use later. Once he had Ireina and Demos, they would have need for money to make good their escape.

He covered his own, too recognizable warrior's garments with a robe of fine green silk from the chest. On his wrists he placed bracelets of gold and silver where they could be seen easily. Once he had finished with his costume, he was ready. The lamp was extinguished, plunging the room back into darkness.

He returned to the empty streets. In the distance, he could hear the howling of a dog, punctuated by the pealing of bells from the cathedrals. Low wisps of mist rose from the stones of the streets and gutters and were moved gently by the night air. Pulling up the hood of his new robe, he quickly retraced his steps to the place of the eunuch Gregory. If the sentries there were like most, the changing of the guard would not take place for at least another two hours. That was all the time he would have. It should be enough. The stench of decay walked with him, permeating the damp air blown in from the Bosphorus.

Finding his original position by the walls, Casca moved close to the gate. There wasn't any way for him to get over the walls

without aid. He would have to come in from the front. He tried
to make himself smaller. Twisting his shoulders and walking
with stiff heavy steps, he kept his face averted from the glow of
the torch in an iron bracket by the barred gate to Gregory's palace. In the flickering of the flame, he could see eyes watching
his approach from an archer's aperture in the watch gate.

Stumbling forward, he half collapsed. Beating at the door
with a feeble hand, he choked out a weak cry: "Help me, please
let me in. All my family is dead. Let me in." He whimpered, "I
don't want to die." He coughed, raising a hand to his mouth and
letting the gold and silver bracelets sparkle in the glow of the
torch.

He heard a movement behind the walls. Perhaps they needed
a bit more incentive. He fell to his knees; holding his hands
clasped as if in prayer, he begged them to let him in. Fumbling
under his robe, he took out his purse and raised it above his
head, crying out to them: "I have gold and jewels, enough to
make you rich men for the rest of your lives. If only you'll let
me in; it's all yours, take it all." He sobbed, turning the sack
upside down to let the coins of gold and silver fall in a bright
rain to the ground as his body shook and shuddered. He had
seen death come enough times to know the symptoms.

The sounds behind the wall had increased when he opened
the purse. He knew that he had their attention. Now for the coup
de grace. Casca fell face forward to the wall, hands outstretched. He cried, "I have more much more on me; it's all
yours." He doubled himself over as if cramps were tearing at
his abdomen. From his throat came the sounds of choking. His
body went into a convulsive spasm and then was still.

Behind the wall, the two sentries argued over what they
should do. They knew that it meant death for them to let anyone
from the outside in. But the man outside was dead, and the gold
he carried would be taken by some filthy slaves if they didn't
take it for themselves first. Surely there could be no harm if they
opened the gate for just enough time to strip the body. No one
would ever be the wiser as long as they kept their mouths shut.
And there was enough to split between them that they might be
able to get out of the city and find safety for themselves, away
from the plague.

Casca could hear the sound of the gate being unlatched and
then a thin squeak as the door opened just enough to permit one
of the two sentries inside to squeeze his body out. He held his

breath. Beneath his robe, his sword was already drawn. He would need it to keep the gate from being shut on him.

The guard took a quick look left and right down the street to make sure there was no one out to tell of this later; then he moved quickly to what he thought was the body. Reaching over to remove the bracelets from the wrists of the corpse, he felt a hand grasping his own wrist, holding it in a vise, as a weak trembling voice came from the dead man: "Help me, please."

The guard tried to pull away, standing back up. As he did, he pulled the plague victim to his feet with him. The weight of the sick man leaned against him, forcing him back against the gate. The guard tried to move his hand to where he could draw his sword, but the power of the diseased man's grip threatened to break his wrist. The two stumbled against the gate, and the guard called for his friend inside to come and help him.

"Get this crazy son of a bitch off me! Kill him!"

There was no need to ask his comrade to come out; Casca was ready to go in. He stuck his sword blade in the small opening remaining in the gate to prevent it from being closed. He shifted his grip from the wrist to the throat, placing the thumb down low on the esophagus, the fingers sinking deep into the thick muscles of the broad strip of meat that ran from the base of the head to the shoulder. Twisting, he forced the man's head back into an off angle, forcing the sentry's body around until it lost balance, forcing him to his knees, where his face met the knee of the man he had come to rob. Casca dropped him and hit the door with his shoulder, forcing it open, driving back the man who was holding it.

He shouldered his way through, one hand grabbing the guard's throat to choke off any outcry, the other driving the sword into the belly between the scaled plates of armor, entering the large artery running along the spine. He let the body drop to drain on the earth.

He was inside. Now to find someone who could tell him where his woman and child were being held. Then he would tend to Brother Gregory. Gregory's palace was of two stories, surrounding a central park with fountains and Greek statuary. Twice he heard the voices of sentries patrolling the grounds in pairs. Laying low in decorative bushes, he let them pass.

Moving to a window that had been left open to allow the night air to circulate, he climbed over a low balustrade and dropped down to a long hall, wishing he knew more about the layout of the house. But if it went according to plan, the master's rooms would be on the second floor, where he could take advantage of the night breeze, with his aide or secretary in a room close to him. That's where he would go: the second floor.

Staying close to the walls, he tried to blend in with the shadows in the darkened interior of the palace. At junctions, there were lamps of oil swinging from censures overhead, but not many. The master was a frugal person, and oil was expensive.

He paused at each door, listened, and moved on to the next. At the room next to the end of the hallway, a rustle came through the carved oak door. He waited, trying to hold down the pounding of his heart in his ears. He wondered where the rest of the household guards were. There had to be more of them around than he had seen.

Gingerly, he tried the latch. To his relief, it turned easily. Holding his breath, he opened it enough to permit entry and slid sideways inside, sword to the front. Nothing other than the thin grumbling of someone in a troubled sleep reached his ears.

Silently, he moved into the interior of the room. A light breeze rustled curtains by an open window, letting a dim glow seep through to cast a pale light by which he saw a figure in sleep on the couch, one arm thrown over his eyes, knees drawn up nearly to the chest. He moved closer, careful to make no sound to wake the sleeper before he was ready. He looked down on the face of the fair-haired man. Timoteus rolled over to his side, straightened his legs, and mumbled in his sleep. Casca hoped he was having an unpleasant dream so that what was going to happen to him in the next few minutes might not prove to be too much of a shock.

He exchanged his sword for the dagger. It was handier when working in close, though he knew it was unlikely that he would need it to handle the sleeper. His hands were able to do the job, with the strength in the fingers that had grasped the oars of a slave galley for longer than this sleeper had lived.

One hand covered Timoteus's throat. Casca squeezed; it was a gentle squeeze, but it was enough that no sound could issue from the sleeper's mouth when his eyes opened and tried to focus in terror, not really certain that he wasn't still dreaming. If this wasn't a nightmare, it deserved to be one, especially when he caught a look at the face of the man holding him pinned to his bed.

Casca eased the pressure on the throat. He didn't want

Timoteus to pass out. Moving his grip so that he had a thick finger dug into the tender nerves under the ear, he whispered, "Your name?"

Timoteus started to call for help, but a warning squeeze that threatened to crush the cartilage of his throat made him think better of it. He changed in midvoice from a would-be yell to a thin, tiny whisper. "Timoteus, secretary to the—"

Casca was pleased at the answer. He jerked the man out of his bed.

Timoteus nearly screamed when his face hit the floor. A crushing weight on his spine and the point of a dagger at his throat reminded him that he wasn't to make any noise.

He couldn't see his attacker, but after the first question, he had no doubt about who it was.

"Where are my son and wife?" the voice hissed. "Tell me the truth and live. Lie to me, and I'll rip your heart out."

Timoteus tried to answer but found that his throat had suddenly gone as dry as the desert. Desperately, he tried to salivate. This was assisted when the point of the dagger sunk an eighth of an inch into the flesh behind his ear.

Bleatingly, he came to a decision. "You promise that you'll let me live if I tell you the truth?" he whined.

Casca cursed him and agreed to the terms. "Tell me where they are and you'll live. This I promise."

Timoteus held his breath a moment, trying to figure out the best way to tell the story. "Remember," he wheedled, "you promised."

Impatient, Casca prodded him with the point of the dagger. "Keep stalling much longer and you won't live long enough to keep your end of our bargain. Tell me now!"

The acolyte realized that he had no choice in the matter and was convinced that if he lied, he would die. "Your woman is in a room to the rear of the master's. There is no way to reach her without going through his chambers first. She is unharmed."

Casca prodded him again. "And my son; where is he?"

He took longer to answer this, but the feel of blood running down the back of his neck from his punctured mastoid made his mind up for him. "He is dead." Spurting the words in a rush, he blurted, "The Elder killed him to see if he was the same as you, to see if he would truly die."

Pain struck Casca's chest, stopping the beat of his heart as the shock of the words took effect. The blood drained from his face, leaving him cold inside. He pushed the point of the dagger in a bit farther, resisting the urge to rip open his prisoner's neck. "Do you mean that Gregory has killed my son, or did one of you pieces of shit do it?"

Timoteus squealed in terror. "It was Gregory. I swear by the sacred blood of Jesus, it was Gregory who killed him. No one else touched the boy."

The cherubic face of Demos swam before his eyes, the bright smile and soft gentle lips of his child.

He rolled him over to look at the man's eyes. The hate in his voice came from deep inside his chest, exhaled with his every breath. "You have killed my son for no reason!"

Timoteus saw his death in Casca's eyes as the dagger was raised over him.

Tears burst from his eyes as he sobbed out, "You promised I wouldn't die. You promised me if I told the truth, you would let me live."

Casca cut off his protests with a death grip around his throat, holding him firmly to the stone floor as his knife descended. He responded to Timoteus's pleadings just before the knife entered the acolyte's chest: "Sometimes I lie." He ripped him open from the navel to the sternum. Rising from the body, Casca stumbled against the wall, resting his head against the marble facing.

Pain, anguish from the guilt he knew was his, that Demos had died because of him, drove him to the brink of madness. Tears flowed unchecked down his face. Only the thought that Ireina still lived and needed him kept him from turning into a screaming maniac. Ireina! She was still alive. He had to save her. That came first; then he would punish every member of the Brotherhood who crossed his path. He would hunt them down until they were exterminated. There would be mercy shown. No plea of innocence would be heard. They had condemned themselves by their words and actions. They would die!

He had to step over the body to reach the door. The acolyte's face would be buried with the look of terror that was already indelibly impressed on his features.

Stumbling, Casca returned to the hallway, moving to the next large room at the end of the hall, where large double doors of hardwood, embossed with castings of copper in bas-relief, stood between him and Gregory. Sucking in a deep breath, he took several steps back and hurled his body forward. The double doors burst open as the lock broke inward.

Gregory rose from behind his desk at the crash of his door. Startled, he knocked his chair over, rising to his feet. His bodyguards reacted swiftly to the intrusion, moving to place themselves between the intruder and their master.

Gregory froze everyone in place with an imperious command: "Stay!" He'd recognized his unannounced guest.

Casca stood still, face pale and sweating, every fiber of his body trembling in rage.

Gregory was quick to regain his composure. "Welcome, Casca Longinus. I have been expecting you. You have made good time." He saw the knuckles of Casca's sword hand turn white on the grip of his sword, a contrast to the brighter stains of blood covering much of his arms and tunic.

Stiff-legged, Casca stepped forward till he was halted by Gregory's upraised hand.

"Please remain where you are. Come at me, and your woman will die. My men will slit her throat from ear to ear. Surely you wouldn't want that on your conscience?"

Casca believed him as he saw the door indicated by Gregory's pointing finger open a crack and then close, followed by the sound of strong bolts being rammed shut.

Confident, the Elder moved nearer to face the man he had sought for such a long time.

"I see that you have been busy living up to your reputation."

Casca didn't respond.

"Well, never mind. We have more important things to consider. I know that you are consumed with burning curiosity to know why I have gone to such extremes to bring you here. It is really very simple and the essence of logic." Gregory paused for effect and returned to his desk, sitting back down. He braided his fingers under his chin before continuing. "You have by now of course realized that I am the Elder of the Brotherhood, and as such, I have certain duties to perform. One of these is to keep track of you. In the last century, that has been exceedingly difficult. I propose to change that. You will stay with us, or if you do go anywhere, you will be accompanied by a member of our order. By this means we shall be assured that when the day of the return occurs, we shall be there to greet the master."

Gregory carefully refrained from making any reference to Demos. "In return for your cooperation, we shall keep your woman and the child safe and in comfort.''

Casca tried to think clearly. He shook his head to clear the blood film from his mind. ''How do I know for certain that you have Ireina and she is alive? You know what I am, and if you can't prove what you say, then you also know that I will kill every one of you I can get, too. For the first time I can think of, the curse of Jesus is to my advantage. Show me my wife now, or I will accept it as a fact that she is dead, and all here shall join her.''

Gregory hadn't expected this turn of thought. Casca did not have a reputation for being much of a thinker. The child was dead, true, but he could keep that a secret and use the child's whereabouts as a lever to keep the beast in line. It was also true that they couldn't kill Casca, but he could be chained and in that manner controlled once he submitted.

CHAPTER FIFTEEN

Search

Gregory nodded his head. "I agree. You will be shown the woman, but not the child just yet. Not until we have reached an agreement about your future conduct." He called out loudly enough for the men in the next room to hear. "Bring the woman out to me."

Casca held his breath, waiting for the door to open. When it did, a sweaty chill ran over him. What could he say? Did she know about Demos? He didn't know if he had the strength to tell her that their son was dead. He feared that it would drive her mad.

The door swung open. Ireina was escorted into the larger room by two armed guards. The first was armed with a javelin, the other with a dagger held to her back, his other hand holding a thin leather leash about her neck. She didn't look as if she had been hurt.

When she saw Casca, she cried out to him, "I knew you would come and free us."

"Free us," she had said. That meant she didn't know about Demos. The guard jerked her leash to silence her. She started to move instinctively but was halted by the dagger in her captor's hand, now moving to touch her throat.

Casca pointed his own weapon at the castrato. "Touch her and I'll rip your arm off." He directed his next words to Gregory. "You know I can do it, and you can't stop me." His words lowered to the point where they were barely audible, spoken from the back of his throat with such hate that it startled even Gregory. "I know what you are, and I know what you have done. Do you really think that I could let you go on breathing?"

Gregory stuttered, confused by the turn of events. "What do you mean? What I have done?"

Casca moved a step closer, his face pale, the pores open, letting the sweat of hate collect to run down his face.

"You have killed my son. The only chance I will give you is if you free my woman now. I'll take her away, but then I'm going to come back and butcher you as I would a hog."

Gregory was suddenly very frightened by what he had brought into his home. It took some effort to face the absolute loathing in Casca's eyes and manner. "You wouldn't dare do anything to me while I hold your wife."

Casca grunted harshly. "That's true, but remember, she won't live forever. Then what?"

That was another thing Gregory hadn't thought of. What would the beast do when he no longer had his wife as a hostage?

Ireina couldn't make out all the words clearly, but she did hear them say something about her son. She struggled against the guard holding her, causing him to nearly lose his grip and in anger push the point of his dagger a bit into her throat, causing her to give a cry of pain.

Casca screamed at the guard, taking a step toward him and raising his sword. "I told you what I would do." His advance was halted by the guard with the javelin, who panicked when Casca moved.

Ireina saw the man's hand draw back, preparing for a cast at her man. She stamped her heel against the instep of the guard holding her, breaking free of him to rush between the javelin and Casca. The barbed head took her squarely between the shoulders, piercing the lungs and heart. She was dead before she hit the ground.

That was the final straw. Casca broke. He rushed at the brave member of the Spathos-cublicar, his sword splitting the man's chest open as if he wore no armor.

Gregory screamed like a panicked woman. "What have you done?" he cried. He shouted for the other guard to stop Casca as he threw himself into the doorway leading to his bed chambers and bolted it behind him. He had to get away.

Casca cried out to him, "It will do you no good to run. I'll find you no matter where you go. I will kill you and those with you. There is no place for you to hide from me.''

Gregory missed the last of his words, as he was already out of his rooms and heading down a passageway to the outside, where he could reach the rest of his household guard and get away.

Casca stopped, chest heaving, eyes swollen red, the muscles in his chest and neck swollen near the bursting point. He moved close to the guard who had held his dagger at Ireina's neck. ''I told you what I would do to you,'' he whispered.

The castrato in gilded armor knew that he was going to die. Terror turned his legs to water. The dagger dropped from his hand to the floor. He tried to find his tongue to beg for mercy but couldn't; the words stuck in his throat. He was going to die, and there was no escape for him. Casca's sword dropped to the floor.

The guard whimpered as scarred hands connected. Twisted, heavily muscled arms took him, raised him from the floor, and hammered him down against the cool marble. He couldn't breathe. The air had been forced from his lungs, and his head had nearly cracked open. He was confused, terrified, unable to do anything. What was happening? His right arm was held by the hands of the man who was killing him, pulling it up. A foot held against his shoulder provided the leverage Casca needed. He began to twist and turn the arm at the shoulder. First it dislocated, the tendons tearing as the muscles separated, stretching. The guard found his voice long enough to scream. Then he fainted when he heard the flesh tear as Casca twisted the arm around and around, jerking at it, using all the strength in his back and shoulders. At last the flesh and skin gave way. In long, stringy, red and white strands the meat shredded as Casca pulled the arm from the guard's shoulder.

Casca usually tried to do what he said he would. He tossed the limp stump into a corner. Now he had other prey on his mind. Gregory was outside somewhere. It was time to pay the rest of his bill. He looked at the small body of Ireina and wept in misery, accusing himself aloud: ''I knew that I should not have taken you with me. I bring nothing but death and pain to those I love. Forgive me.''

He left her where she was; there was no more he could do for her. Now he had to do something for himself. He wanted the Elder, and he was going to have him if he had to kill a thousand men to reach him. He would have the Elder of the Brotherhood, and all who stood in his way did so at their own peril. He at last had good reason to live. He would live so that he could kill!

Gregory had thrown himself onto the saddle of a horse when he'd heard the guard upstairs scream. He knew that Casca was living up to his word. Panic-stricken, he whipped his horse out of the gates, riding blindly to the nearest exit from the city. There was only one place he could go where he might get help. He had to reach Narses at his camp in the Valley of Olives.

Casca was detained for only a moment by another of Gregory's guards who'd rushed in when he heard the sound of screaming. The guard had lousy timing. Casca left him spitting blood from a punctured lung on the stone staircase. He reached the walls surrounding the palace in time to hear the hoofbeats of Gregory's horse heading east. He didn't waste time returning to the gate he had entered through. This time he went straight over the wall on the east side and dropped down into the street. He ran after the sound of the fading hooves.

Near the Hagia Sofia, he ran head on into a mounted patrol of four imperial sentries. Jerking the nearest of them off his animal, he put himself in the seat without stopping, racing on in the direction Gregory had taken. He would find him. It was just a matter of time, and for once that was to his advantage. He knocked out the guard at the east gate when he rode over him. The man's back was turned to him as he wondered what was so important to cause the magister to ride out in such a hurry.

Gregory whipped the flanks of his horse to get every last ounce of speed out of him. It was dawn when he reached the camp of Narses, who tried to talk him in to staying with him and his Sparthos-cublicar. They would protect him. But Gregory would have none of it, crying that Narses didn't know what he was talking about. They weren't dealing with an ordinary man. He was being chased by Satan himself. The only chance he had was to run.

Narses gave in to his master and assigned him an escort of ten of his Spathos, who were all members of the Brotherhood. They would protect him till he reached safety. And if Gregory didn't get away, who could say how far he, Narses, would advance in the ranks of the Brotherhood and the empire?

Casca was in a grove of olive trees when he saw Gregory and

his escort ride out of the camp of the eunuchs, still heading east. His stolen horse was not good for much more, but that didn't matter. If he had to travel every yard on foot, he knew that he would one day catch up to the Elder. He would follow him to the most distant reaches of the world and beyond. He had to. The blood of those who had loved him forced him on, calling to him in the night, crying out to him to avenge their deaths.

"Run, Gregory, run."

"Death is not far behind. Just look over your shoulder and I'll be there."

He followed after them, never able to catch up to Gregory, but he did take care of the members of the Spathos whom Gregory had left behind to slow him. They were nothing, merely an appetizer before the main course. The only direction he wouldn't go was back. There was nothing for him there.

His trail was marked by the bodies he'd left behind. The questions he asked at villages and farms were always answered. No one refused him anything. The madness that lay in his eyes loosened reluctant tongues. He looked much like the madmen of the desert, who care not whether they eat or drink, taking only enough to sustain them, no more.

There was no pleasure for him in anything. Neither was there any pain, save for the voices of Demos and Ireina that walked with him through the deserts and rocky valleys of his path. They whispered to him on the wind, and in his few hours of sleep, they would come to him to relive the brief moments they'd had of sharing. Demos's childish laughter rode with him on the barren sands. Several times he would stop and look around to see where Demos was. He knew from the laughter that the boy was near him, just out of reach or sight. Perhaps over the next hill he would find him playing and laughing, waiting for Casca to come and put him on his broad shoulders, where he would giggle and laugh when they ran and played together.

Several times in the next weeks, when Casca did look back the way he had come, he saw a distant figure on horseback, always keeping his distance, never coming too close. He knew it was always the same one behind him, but it didn't matter. As long as his shadow stayed to the rear, it wouldn't slow him. After he finished Gregory, he would take care of the one following him.

He lost track of time and distance; only the trail of Gregory drew him back from the borders of madness.

When he had ridden his horse to death, after missing the last waterhole, he went on another ten miles before passing out. When he woke, there was half a skin of water lying by his side. The tracks of a horse leading to and from him meant that his shadow was still with him, and it was not an enemy. He thanked his benefactor silently and drank from the skin. Now he could go on.

From a hill, he looked across the valley of the Chazari. The other side led to the heartlands of Persia. Once more he would have to go east, into lands that were hostile and filled with memories of things best forgotten. But he would go, for that was where Gregory was.

Below, in the valley, a great storm was gathering, rolling across the barren floor of scrub brush and stone, a white cloud, its fringes touched with blood from the setting sun. The cloud advanced. Under normal circumstances he would have waited it out before going on, but not now. He could let nothing stop him; somewhere in front of him was Gregory. He had to go on.

Tying a scrap of cloth around his face to filter the sand, he pulled the hood of his burnoose over his head as he began the descent to the floor of the valley. Walking straight to meet the advancing cloud, head down, eyes on the ground, he met the first blast of wind. He ignored the small bites of whipping grains that had ridden the wind all the way from the endless sands of Arabistan.

The cloud rolled over him. The small stinging bites changed suddenly into a raging storm that tried to strip the meat from his body, leaving only bare bones to mark his passing, as they had already done to several hundred others who had been caught in the path of the winds.

He fought through drifts that suddenly appeared from out of the cloud to drag at him, pulling at his feet like dry quicksand. Cursing all the gods of creation, he pushed forward one step at a time, detaching his mind from all else, thinking only of the next step, always one step more. He knew that as long as he faced the wind, he was heading in the right direction. His mind pulled away as it narrowed its concentration onto those two factors. One more step and face the wind, head down, body hunched over.

He didn't feel the raw spots opening on the exposed portions of his cheeks as the sand wore away the skin to the raw meat. There was no bleeding; the heat of the wind and sand clotted the wounds as fast as they were made. He was aware only of a distant burning sensation in his face. He didn't care if the sand ground its way clear through the meat of his face and head, leaving him only a white polished skull, as long as he could keep moving.

Insidiously, individual grains worked through the threads of his robes to gather in hard grinding knots in his armpits and groin till each separate movement of his arms joined with the distant burning of his face. He knew he was hurting, but he had known greater pain than this. It wouldn't kill him. If he'd had any humor left, he would have laughed at this last thought.

The storm rolled over him, passing on to some unknown infinity where it would disappear without any trace of ever having been. Rising from his knees, he stood covered with dust. A ghostly figure in the evening sun, eyes nearly glued shut, face, hands, every pore caked and covered with the white dust. Spitting on his fingers to clean them, he wiped his eyes clear enough to focus on the scene below.

It took some time for him to see that what he was looking at was not some city of a forgotten ancient era, abandoned and left to the winds that still blew over the surface of the desert lake and spotted with islands of white on which columns and blocks stood. Stumbling forward, he made each step his next goal in life, to reach the shimmering waters that beckoned him, only to find what he already knew. When he reached them, they would be too salty to drink.

This was one of the lakes left by a retreating sea, and now it served as a depository for salt beds. Each year the lake shrunk a bit more, the sun and wind evaporating the waters, leaving an ever-increasing degree of salt in the water and on the dry beds that the water had abandoned.

Reaching the edge of the salt lake, he waded waist deep into the brine. If he couldn't take the water into his mouth, he would let his pores soak in what they could. At least it would rinse off more than it left on him of the alkaline residue. He put his face under the surface to rinse his hair and upper body, shutting his eyes tight against the salt, which he knew could drive a man mad if he took to much of it into himself.

When he rose from the waters, the sun evaporated the moisture from the surface of his skin within seconds. His eyes cleared a bit. He saw movement about him in the thick waters. Thousands, no, millions of tiny forms that flickered with changing colors in the water, where nothing should be able to live. Tiny, wriggling creatures by the uncounted millions swam and swirled in vast herds. Most had a reddish tinge. He wondered if they were edible.

Dredging himself out of the water, Casca walked the perimeter of the lake, coming upon the carcasses of dead birds by the dozens and a few animals of the four-legged variety. All were covered by alkali and salt dust. The birds nearest the edge of the water felt spongy to the touch; those farther away, the older corpses, were as hard as marble, frozen in a crust of white death. He touched his own hair and beard. They too were acquiring the same sponginess.

Shading his eyes with his right hand, he scanned the horizon. On the north corner of the lake bed, he saw blocks of salt piled high near a mound of stones that didn't have a natural look. He moved to them, lungs aching, sucking in the dry salty air. As he neared, he saw that the blocks were man-cut chunks and that the stones formed a crude hut. This was one of the places where, periodically, slave or even migrant tribesmen would camp. He saw no sign of life around the hut. Still, he exercised a degree of caution. Taking his sword from the scabbard, he tried to move with more sureness than he felt.

Casca was about a quarter mile away when he saw a figure break away from the hut and run over a small rocky rise to the north. It reminded him of his shadow. He turned to look back the way he had come. There he was, looking as if he were drifting in the air on heat waves.

Casca broke into a lope. He wanted to run faster but wasn't capable of it. Reaching the hut, he climbed the stones to the roof and looked to the north. A man was riding away on a leg-weary horse, whipping the animal with frantic lashes.

Climbing back down, he stumbled, slipping on the uneven stones. His face struck a boulder, breaking his mouth open to let the salty taste of his blood mingle with the salt dust in his breath. Wearily, he pulled back up to his feet and entered the uncovered entrance of the hut. It took a second for his eyes to adjust to the change in light from the glare outside.

The hut was only about ten feet in diameter. Piled in the corner, what he thought at first glance to be a pile of rags and rubble proved to be the bodies of three men and a woman. All were dead. The men had had their throats slit, and the woman looked as if her neck had been snapped.

Nosing around, he found a skin of rancid water under the bodies. The rest of the hut had been cleaned out of anything to eat. It was hard to get his thoughts organized. He knew that he was smart enough to figure out what happened, but the thought just wouldn't take cohesive form in his mind.

Removing the wood plug from the skin, he drank, careful not to spill even the smallest drop. The rancid, stinging water was ambrosia. It was shocking, the amount of pure pleasure he felt when the moisture cut through the sticky salty film that covered the inside of his mouth and gums. He had to fight the temptation to drink too deeply.

Moving one of the bodies over to make room, he sat down, removing his burnoose to let his body breathe. The sun was nearly setting. He could feel inside the hut the minute differences in temperature, but it would be several hours before the stored heat in the stones gave way to the chill of the high desert nights. When that happened, he would go on.

Flies were beginning to gather, drawn to the blood on the throats of the dead. He covered the wounds with scraps of their clothing and closed his mind to the nagging, irritating droning.

The water he'd drunk began to have some effect, helping to clear the muck away from his mind so that thoughts came through in some order again. The hut and its dead occupants were most probably a family of salt cutters.

Who had killed them? He didn't move from where he was sitting but let his eyes do the searching. On the dusty floor were the imprints of many feet. Several of the prints were from fine, smooth-soled sandals, not from rough, calloused, bare feet or twisted fibers tied together. Bending over to look closer, he could see the marks of fine even stitching. The sandals were not those of a poor man or even a nomadic tribesman. No nomad would wear shoes so fine in a country like this; they just wouldn't last long enough. He shook his head violently from side to side to aid the slow thinking process. He knew all the answers but couldn't get them out in order fast enough.

When it all came together, he felt like a moron, for he had

known the answer all the time. Gregory had been here. Now, why had one of his men remained behind?

It took some grinding of his gears, but he came up with a logical solution. The man was bait. He had been watching for Casca and had intentionally let himself be seen riding away, to lure him away from the path of Gregory and the others. Or maybe the man had run away when Gregory had left him behind, because he wanted no more of the killer who was hunting them.

That presented Casca with a problem. He didn't want to lose any time catching up with Gregory, but the man they'd left behind did have a horse. What shape the horse was in he didn't know. He might lose time going after the single rider, but if he did catch him, he would gain the added pleasure of being able to kill him, even if the horse wasn't any good or had already died. Besides, he had a strong suspicion where Gregory was heading. He would gamble. Uncorking the goatskin again, he drank a toast to himself, pleased at his shrewdness.

He hesitated a moment, trying to force his reluctant brain to obey orders. He had been in this part of Persia more than once while in the service of Shapur II. He had never been to this salt lake, but the memory of being told about it returned. He knew the countryside, and if the Brother on the horse kept heading north, he would come to a region of volcanic rocks and rubble that stretched for fifty miles. There a man on foot would be able to move faster than one on horseback. Thumping his head to speed his thoughts, he went back outside to look at the countryside with fresh eyes and mind.

On the horizon, in the glow of the dying sun, were the mountains of the Chorasmia. He was west and south of it; that meant the lava flows were only a night's march to the north. He began to laugh, tickled with the idea that he would be able to kill another one of the bastards. It was good to have a purpose in life!

Not now, though. He would wait a while, knowing that his speed would be better if he slept a couple of hours.

The snorting of a horse woke him. Cautiously, he unsheathed his sword, sneaking out of the hut to find a horse tied to a piece of scrub brush. He touched the sides of the animal and the saddle. His hand came away with a stain. He smelled it. Blood. The explanation for this unexpected gift was clear. His shadow had gone after the runaway and had brought back his horse.

Again he gave thanks to the one who followed after him. Now he could make up for lost time and get a little closer to the object of all his desires.

CHAPTER SIXTEEN

Vengeance Is Mine

The warm days were giving way to the first thin flakes of snow to fall from the high lands of Sogdiana, to the borders of the Persia and the northern regions, where the hordes of Asia lay in wait, renewing their strength for another move to the west. They were patient; if not this century, it would be the next. He looked down from the same rise where first he had laid eyes on the sanctuary of the Brotherhood of the Lamb. Then there had been a young boy of the tribes of the Yueh-chih with him, named Jugotai. Then there had been a distant glow from a flame to guide his final steps. Now there was only darkness, but he knew that they were there. He could feel them.

He didn't like this place. The memories of his last visit were not pleasant. It was here that he had first come into contact with the mad followers of Izram, the thirteenth disciple, and the beginning of a private war that had followed him through the ages. He rose to stand in his stirrups, looking over the countryside. Here the Jaxartes still turned from the mountains to flow to the Aral Sea. Nearby, the silk road ran from the Great Wall to the west, carrying the wealth of the East.

He had that strange feeling of things that repeat themselves: the short hoarse bark of a desert jackal, the rustle of brush in the night wind. Kicking his horse in the flanks, he began his descent to the floor of the valley, taking his time. There was no longer any need to hurry. Those waiting below would not run any farther; this he knew. There was nowhere else for them to go. In the shadows, the lines of the walls of the sanctuary became visi-

ble. Massive, silent, forboding, the cathedral had been carved
out of the living stone of the basalt walls of the gorge. Before
reaching bottom, he looked to his rear. It'd been a week or more
since last he had seen his guardian angel. Maybe he had gotten
lost. It didn't matter.

Stopping out of bow range, he dismounted, letting the reins
of his horse drop to the earth. The animal whinnied through red-
membraned nostrils, sore from days of breathing thin dry air.
Unsheathing his sword with his right hand, he also let slip the
strap holding the ax to his side. This he hefted in his left hand as
he neared the ruins of a massive door that bore the mutilated
sign of the fish. This time there would be no Elder Dacort to offer him drugged food and drink. The only thing he would feed
on this time was the pain and blood of those who had taken Demos and Ireina from him.

The odor of long years of disuse was plain. A pack rat ran by
his feet from out of the brush piled in the doorway by the desert
winds. He paused to listen, to taste with his mind the aura of the
sanctuary. Kneeling down, he carefully scanned the loose sand
and dirt that had drifted into the open door. He smiled stiffly.
He was right; they were here. The surface of the sand had been
swept with a piece of leafy brush to wipe out their footprints,
but the evidence of their passing was clear. With the sweeping,
they had left patterns on the surface that could not have occurred
naturally. He nearly wept with joy. Soon they would pay. Then
perhaps the torment that had driven him these last months would
ease.

His left wrist ached with a ghost pain when he entered the
broken doors. The air inside the temple was heavy with the must-
iness of time and disuse. One step, then another. Inside, to
where the only light came from a cold moon whose rays sometimes found cracks in the broken roof to peek through. It was all
different shades of gray: gray stones, gray shadows, gray dust.
He stopped to listen. He could hear something coming from
down the hall. He knew what was there: the altar, where his
spear had been worshiped as a holy relic for centuries. Absent-
ly, he wondered if they still had it. Not that it made any difference now.

As he neared, he saw a thin glow of gold under the door to the
main hall. They were waiting for him. Maybe Gregory was tired
of running and had come here to die at the first home of the

Brotherhood. Casca wouldn't have thought the followers of Izram were so sentimental.

As he neared the doors, they swung open from the inside. Torches in brackets illuminated the interior where once the Brotherhood had knelt to pray. Near the old altar, facing him, was Gregory. On either side of him stood two of the Spathos with bared swords. Removing his loose Arab robe, he let it slide to the dusty stones.

Gregory had lost weight. Gone was the fleshy face of one who had always eaten well. He was much leaner and stronger looking. The months on the trail had hardened him considerably in the body. Casca looked closely at his face. What was it he saw there? Resignation? Acceptance of the inevitable? He couldn't tell. The eunuch warriors of the Spathos had no such look. Their eyes were hard and the grip on their weapons sure. Four of them? When he had started out after them, there had been ten. He'd killed four, and his mysterious shadow had probably killed the one whose horse he rode. There should have been another one, unless he had died or gone on from here to somewhere else. Whichever condition was true was all right with him. The important thing was that right now he was within reach of Gregory.

The ax in his left hand began to swing back and forth. Gregory watched the ax as beads of sweat broke out on his forehead. The Spathos did nothing. Speaking for the first time, Gregory found his throat dry and the words hard to say.

"Is there no other way? What could the boy have meant to you? You were not his real father, and they would have died anyway. Surely you, more than anyone else, must know how truly unimportant are the lives of people like them. Their bodies would be turned to dust for ages, and you would still be the same. What are a couple of more deaths to you, who have put uncounted numbers in that state?"

Casca watched him as he would have a vulture. "Everything you say has some truth to it. The boy was not of my blood. But I loved him as if he were. The woman loved me, and that was enough. However, I am pleased that you put such a low value on mortal life. It should make your own death a bit easier for you to accept."

Gregory glanced at his remaining guards. "I know we can't kill you. But I also know that you can be hurt. If you are hurt badly enough, you won't recover in time to do me any harm. My mistake was sending men at you one at time. I should have just had them overpower you by the sheer force of numbers. But I panicked. I admit it. But no more! Here at this holy place I will still beat you. These four are to be my instruments of deliverance. They are going to hack off your arms and legs. Then I will have total control over you. And if your arms and legs by some means return, why then, they shall simply be removed again and again.''

Casca grinned, letting the heat build up in him. "Then let's do it. Come to me, you precious things. I'll give you a kiss that will last you for the rest of your lives.''

The four separated, each to a different side when Gregory nodded for them to go ahead. They were good, steady fighters who accepted their fate. They knew that some of them would die, perhaps all of them, but that didn't matter as long as they accomplished by their deaths that which the master wished.

Carefully, they began to move in, closing the circle around their prey. They knew that if they wounded him severely enough, they'd have him. Casca didn't let them get too close. He selected the one nearest the side of the hall and went at him, letting loose a scream to give himself strength. He struck out with the sword, going for the eyes, forcing the eunuch to blink by reflex. In that blinking of an eye, the ax in Casca's left hand was already in flight, the heavy, razor-edged blade sinking into the carotid artery, leaving the eunuch's head hanging by some strands of meat and bone at an awkward angle before he fell.

The remaining guards tried to rush Casca as he took out their comrade. He pulled back to the wall, where they couldn't get at him from the back. The eunuchs were good soldiers, but that was all they were. They hadn't the experience to deal with one like him. But then, they were ready to die if they could just get hold of him. The largest of them threw his body at Casca, using it as a shield for the others to come behind. He expected to die, and he did. Casca's sword went through him till the hilt rested against the muscles of his stomach. Before the blade could be pulled out, the other two were on him, slashing and striking. A cut laid his left arm open to the bone: a long, narrow, lengthwise slice from the tip of his shoulder to the elbow. Their attack forced him away from the wall and back into the center of the room, his back to the open altar. It was then he found out where the missing Spathos was.

A cry of "Duck!" coming from the doorway made him drop his body to the floor, twisting around. Hrolvath stood there, a light javelin leaving his hand to fly over Casca's head. It missed its target! The missing Spathos, who had been hiding behind the altar with a bow, didn't miss. The arrow he had intended for Casca flew across the open room to find the chest of Hrolvath. Casca screamed again. This time, if they wanted him down, they would have to chop him into pieces where he stood. He went at the two eunuchs, driving them both back against the wall. He used no finesse in his sword work. It was the rough work of one who slaughtered beasts for a living. He hacked down their guards. Using his sword like a cleaver, he sliced away arms and faces. As long as they stood, he cut and beat at them, mindless of his own wounds; they meant nothing. He ripped them open as a boy guts a fish, leaving a trail of entrails dragging after them.

Gregory couldn't move; he was frozen in horror. The deaths he had participated in before had been those where he was the one in control. There was no controlling this raging animal. The Book of Izram was right. Casca was the spawn of Satan, a devil in the flesh of man, an inhuman thing of blood and death for all who touched him. The death blows given to his guards were the only act of mercy shown. And now, he alone faced this madman, with blood dripping off him from neck to waist, both his own tainted fluid and that of the men he had killed. The beast was coming for him, and he couldn't move or speak. Casca, sword raised above his head, red and dripping with the gore of those he had slaughtered, stumbled drunkenly to him. Gregory managed a weak cry of terror and then fainted.

Casca stood over the unconscious body of the Elder, legs and arms trembling as he sucked in air to feed the furnace of his hate. A moan of pain came to him: Hrolvath! In his passion he had forgotten him. He left Gregory where he was; there would be time for him later.

The feathers were nearly touching the skin. He knelt down beside his young friend to raise his head from the floor, cradling it in his good arm. Hrolvath tried to smile as bubbles of bright blood rose to his lips to burst with each breath.

The madness left Casca as he looked at the face of his friend. "So it was you who were my shadow? Why didn't you ride with me?"

Hrolvath coughed, his lips paling. "I thought you preferred

to be alone, and you might have sent me back. I came after you on the next ship. You were easy to find.'' He coughed again, painfully. ''All I had to do was ask anyone I met if they had seen a madman, and they would point me in the right direction.''

Casca shook his head. ''You should have stayed away. What did it bring you but this?''

Both of them knew that Hrolvath's wound was fatal. The blood on the lips came from his lungs; it was only a matter of minutes or even seconds before his shade would leave his body.

Hrolvath shuddered; his mouth filled with blood. He turned his head to the side to let it drain out. He didn't have the strength to spit it out.

Hrolvath grinned. ''We're sword mates. I couldn't let you go alone. You might have gotten yourself killed.''

Casca laughed bitterly. ''I wish it had been so; then at least you would not have come to this damned place.''

Hrolvath shook his blond head. ''No! Then I would not have been here to save you. That makes it all worthwhile. I . . . have . . . saved you.'' His words faded as his final breath escaped.

Casca lowered his head and stood, looking at the young man who had died believing that he had saved his friend's life. The irony of it brought gales of hysterical laughter. He couldn't stop; he laughed till tears ran in rivers as he cried out to the stones of the hall, ''Did you hear? He died to save my life.''

Gregory moaned, stopping his fit of hysteria. Casca walked quickly over to him and stomped on the side of his head to put him back to sleep. He wasn't ready for him yet. He had things to do before he could give the Elder of the Brotherhood his full attention.

He built a cairn of stone for Hrolvath on a knoll, away from the graves where members of the Brotherhood had been laid to rest in the past. He didn't want Hrolvath near them. When he had laid the last stone, he had one more thing to do. He found his ax and went to look for some trees.

It was past dawn when he prodded Gregory to his feet, legs wavering under the load of the beam. Casca mocked him.

''You want to know what it feels like to die as Jesus did? Then I'll show you, for surely no one could know better than I.''

Pulling up a thorn bush by the roots, he lashed the back of Gregory into bleeding shreds, forcing him up the same path where the Brothers of the Elder Dacort held their reenactments of the crucifixion. Gregory stumbled, falling on his face and breaking his nose. Casca grasped him by the hair to drag him back up to his feet, the beam placed once more on his shoulders.

Gregory sobbed in pain, but there was none of the numbing effect of one lost in religious ecstasy. His was a wail of pain and terror.

Gregory was blinded with blood and tears when they reached the place of death. He had to be stopped by a slap from Casca's hand. He tried to get to his knees, hands clasped in front of him to beg for mercy, only to have his pleas silenced by a fist breaking three of his front teeth, filling his mouth with splinters and blood.

Casca sneered at him. "Mercy? You want mercy? Where was the mercy shown to Demos? Where was the mercy given to Ireina and Hrolvath? I'll give you the mercy you deserve: none! The best I can give you is to let you know what pain truly is."

He forced Gregory to his back to lie with arms outstretched as he was tied to the cross beam by his arms. Casca sweated as he performed a task that he had done only a few times before. But he remembered well. He didn't regret that he had no spikes to puncture Gregory's wrists and feet. It had been a special occasion when they'd done that to Jesus. Pilate hadn't wanted the Jew to live too long.

This time, he would do it as they did in Rome for common criminals. Only the ropes to hold the arms to the beam. No block for the feet to rest on, and one more thing. He stood over Gregory and raised the ax above his head. Turning the blade to the side, he brought it down twice in rapid succession, breaking the bones of the second leg before Gregory could finish screaming from the first.

Leaving him to his pain, Casca went to one of the places where the crosses were dropped into preprepared holes. He had to dig one out, removing some chunks of rotted wood from the last occupant's cross. Once this was done, he dragged Gregory on his cross to where he could begin to raise it. Grasping the head of the cross, he grunted, raising it high enough to get it on his shoulder. Then he began to work his way up the length of it, forcing the cross into an erect position till the foot of it slid into the hole he had prepared. It slid in with a familiar thump, accented by a shrill scream from the Elder.

Once the base of the cross was in place, Casca packed dirt

and rocks around it to hold it firmly. Then he sat back to admire his handiwork. Pleased that he hadn't forgotten how to do the job properly, he turned his attention to Gregory.

"How do you like it? Is it as glorious as you expected? You know, you're luckier than Jesus. You're going to live a lot longer than he did, and you'll know pain that you've never dreamed of. When the swelling starts in your legs and the weight of your body gradually dislocates your shoulders, your own hanging weight will force your lungs to labor harder and harder to get a breath. I have seen men last two days, but I don't think you're that strong. You probably won't go more than ten or twelve hours. So enjoy yourself. I am."

Casca stayed in one spot till sunrise and then rose to stretch his legs. Gregory's screams had been reduced to mewling whimpers. Casca moved a boulder over to stand on and poured water down Gregory's throat to give him strength.

"Not yet! You don't die," he whispered gently. "Not yet!"

Casca talked to him as the heat of the day built, noticing in a detached manner the swelling of Gregory's legs as the blood settled in them, stretching the skin to the point where it was near to bursting.

"You know," he said amiably, "in the old days, it wasn't uncommon to crucify a person head down. That was done when we had a lot to do and didn't have enough crosses to go around. That way most of them died in just an hour or so."

He tapped the point of his sword against the stretched purple skin of Gregory's right leg, just a gentle touch. A dark stream of blood shot forth, propelled by the built-up pressure.

"There! That ought to make you feel a bit better. It'll ease some of the swelling."

The day passed slowly for the man on the cross. Ravens collected on nearby branches to wait as vultures gathered overhead. Casca wondered how the carrion eaters could know when there was going to be food for them and show up before dinner was ready to be served.

Near noon, Gregory forced open his left eye. The other wouldn't move, swollen shut by blood and pus. He tried to force his tongue to move, to make words that came out in a half-dry, rasping whisper. Casca didn't have to hear the words to know what was being said. He walked around the cross, looking over the man, noticing every detail of the manner in which the joints of the shoulders were twisted and distorted out of their sockets. The swelling, where blood vessels had ruptured under the strain, had left red and purple streaks running down the man's chest.

He tested him as a master chef does a fine pastry. He was nearly done. It was time to finish.

Casca stood in front of the cross, looking up at the swollen face of the master of the Brotherhood. "There's one thing yet to be done; then you can go. I'm sorry that I don't have my spear, but I guess that won't make a lot of difference at this point." He drew his sword, placing the point against the skin, just under the last rib on the left side. "I should just leave you for the vultures to finish, but I guess I'm a little selfish. This is one thing I want to do myself."

Gently, taking his time, he slid the sword in, ignoring the sudden burst of blood that spurted forth to cover his arm to the elbow.

In his state of half madness, Casca could feel every vein, nerve, and vessel that his sword cut through. When it touched the heart, he felt a shiver run the length of the steel, transmitting itself to his hand. He hesitated a heartbeat, smiling at Gregory.

"This is it. This is the big one. Hope you appreciate all the trouble I went through for you."

He gave the handle of the sword a gentle push to set the point of his sword into the jerking muscle of the heart. Gregory opened his mouth. A scream came forth to echo over the barren hills, frightening several ravens from their perches, to fly frantically to a safer altitude. Casca wiped the blade on Gregory's loincloth before replacing it in its sheath.

It was done. Perhaps now he could sleep without the voices of those he loved tormenting him with their pain. Slowly, heavily, he left Gregory to the scavengers, not looking back. He found his horse and mounted, turning the animal's head back to the west. He hadn't noticed that the sun was falling and night was once more on the land. He lay over the pommel of the saddle and closed his eyes. In the whisper of the wind, for just a moment before he slept, he thought he heard the tinkling sound of a child's laughter, fading away, being carried on the wind.

The horse carried him, half conscious, exhausted and drained by the curse of his own existence, through canyons of cold stone, reaching over him like the spires of an abandoned city.

The words of the ice cave came to him again:

> *Endlessly weary,*
> *the Silent Sentinel*
> *guards the Tower of Darkness.*
> *Endlessly, endlessly weary.*